THE COMMONER

AND THE

Correspondent

THE
ROYAL AGENTS
OF
MI6

BOOK THREE

USA TODAY BESTSELLING AUTHOR

HEATHER SLADE

THE COMMONER AND THE CORRESPONDENT
© 2021 Heather Slade

Paperback:
ISBN 13: 978-1-953626-37-0

MORE FROM AUTHOR HEATHER SLADE

Table of Contents

1

Pinch

"Bugger me," I seethed when I heard the pub door open and saw the woman coming in.

"Who's that?" asked my best mate, Wilder. He and I had grown up together on his family's estate. Now, we worked together for SIS, Her Majesty's Secret Service—I was with MI5 and he had recently resigned from MI6.

"Bloody reporter," I answered, running my hand over my shortly cropped hair.

"Looks familiar."

"Ms. Cartwright works for the *Times*. She's also friends with your sister."

"She's on her way over here," Wilder warned.

"If there's anyone I'd like to walk into this pub less than the devil himself, it's her."

"Why?"

"She almost brought down my last investigation. Not to mention, she's been snooping around about Wren."

"Bugger me," muttered Wilder, repeating my earlier words and leaving me to join his wife and her brother at their table.

Wren was a former secret agent for the United States National Security Agency, whose identity had been compromised by a leak at the UK's Secret Intelligence Service—otherwise known as MI6. To make matters worse, the security breach had happened while Wilder was serving as the international section's interim chief.

Through the combined efforts of MI6 and MI5, the UK's domestic counterintelligence and security agency, we'd been able to mitigate the threat caused by her exposure. However, the last thing we needed now was someone like Ms. Cartwright poking her nose in it.

Wren and Wilder had both resigned from their respective jobs right after they got married, in order to start a private intelligence consultancy. First, though, they were honeymooning in the Maldives for two weeks. The gathering tonight was to wish the couple a *bon voyage.*

When I heard someone clear her throat, I turned around to find Ms. Cartwright standing directly in front of me.

"Is that Wren Whittaker, or should I say Kennedy King?" she asked, looking beyond me to the table where Wilder and Wren were seated.

I leaned down and got right in her face. "Who she is or isn't, is none of your bloody business. You report one word about anyone in the Whittaker family, and I'll see to it that you're imprisoned for treason—that's if I can't manage to kill you first."

I backed away, folded my arms, and waited for her response.

"Okay, okay. You don't have to be so threaten-y. You know I found out through Darrow."

Darrow. Wilder's younger sister and my former "girlfriend." Although with as many times as we'd been on and off and then on again in the last few months, it was hard to keep track of which we were at any given time.

"Have you found her?" Ms. Cartwright asked, bringing up yet another subject I had no intention of discussing with her.

"No comment."

"Off the record, then. You know she and I have been mates since primary school."

The concern I saw in the woman's eyes was genuine enough that I shook my head.

"She's been gone a week's time now, right?"

To be precise, it had been ten days since Darrow Whittaker disappeared from her residence on the estate that had been in her family for generations, five days since I found her, and three days since she disappeared again, only this time with my help.

Of course, I couldn't talk about any of it with someone outside of her family, especially not a reporter.

"I know how upsetting this must be for you."

I looked down to where her hand rested on my forearm, growling as I wrenched it away. Having concern was one thing; gumshoeing was another.

"The ice you're walking on is exceedingly thin. I suggest you turn around and leave of your own volition, unless you'd prefer I toss you over my shoulder and carry you out."

"Wait, I have another—"

I leaned my shoulder into Ms. Cartwright's stomach and wrapped my arm around the back of her knees. As threatened, I tossed her over my shoulder and carried her out to the pavement.

"What are you doing?" she screeched, pounding on my back. When she tried to kick her legs, I tightened my hold.

I made eye contact with one of several agents also at the pub to bid farewell to Wilder and Wren, who nodded in acknowledgment as I unceremoniously set her feet-first on the pavement in front of the pub.

"Go home!" I spat, turning to go back in. I heard her shout at me to wait, but I ignored her.

Once back inside, I needed a minute before joining the party. I pulled out a stool at the bar, ordered a pint, and took a deep breath. Not the smartest thing I could've done, given the beguiling reporter's scent lingered on my skin.

"I'll take a whiskey as well," I said to the barmaid.

"Looks like you need a double," she responded, setting a glass and the bottle in front of me.

With such close proximity to Vauxhall Cross, otherwise known as SIS headquarters, the pub's staff were trained not to ask questions of their patrons. They did, however, seem to innately know when one of their regulars needed an extra shot or, in this case, two or three.

It wasn't this specific run-in with Ms. Cartwright that had me rattled. I could handle the reporter side of her. It was the female beneath the ink slinger's tough exterior that got under my skin.

I tried my damnedest not to look at her pouty, bee-stung lips or let myself think about how much I wanted to lick off the bright red lipstick she wore.

I raised the glass, inhaling her scent again as I tossed the drink back. The woman smelled like none other I'd ever known—as mysterious and provocative as spicy and floral.

Today her long sandy-blonde hair was pulled back from her face in a tight bun. She wore a dark-colored pencil skirt that skimmed her knees, a loose-fitting white silk blouse that did nothing other than accentuate her mouthwatering curves, and the sexiest damn black heels I'd ever seen.

Having her in my arms, albeit slung over my shoulder, almost did me in. I longed to take her home, strip her bare, and linger over every scrumptious inch of the body that so regularly invaded my dreams.

"Bugger me," I muttered as I had when she walked through the door earlier. Esland Cartwright wasn't just an annoying reporter on my beat, she was one of Darrow's best mates, and that meant hands off.

2

Esland

"Dammit," I muttered when Pinch stalked inside, leaving me in the street.

I'd been staked out nearby when I saw him walk into the pub, but instead of telling him why I needed to talk to him, I got sidetracked when I saw Wren Whittaker.

Now I'd lost my chance. If I tried to go back in, the agent I saw nod at Pinch would prevent me from doing so.

Even when Pinch glared at me, like he had earlier, I couldn't help my body's reaction to the man.

His back had been to me when I approached, giving me a few seconds to take in the way his trousers hugged his sculpted gluteus maximus while his dress shirt strained across his traps, lats, and delts.

When he'd turned toward me and those eyes that seemed brown one minute, blue the next, and the worst, when they looked a perfectly panty-melting shade of sea green, settled on me, I'd almost collapsed in his arms.

Now I was outside and he was in, and as badly as I needed his help, I had no way to get it.

3

Pinch

"Cor blimey," I mumbled the expression I'd pick up from my father when I saw Esland walk back into the pub an hour later. This time, I intended to ignore her. I turned my back, pretending to be part of the conversation.

"Incoming," muttered Wilder.

I took a deep breath and turned around, ready to tear into her. Instead, my eyes met hers, and in them, I saw terror.

"Don't you dare carry me out again," Esland said, holding up both hands while tears welled in her eyes.

I took her arm and led her in the opposite direction of the door. "What's happened?"

She yanked her arm from my grasp. "My flat... someone broke in."

"Was anything taken?"

"I didn't go inside."

"Right." That was actually smart on her part. "Did you ring the peelers?"

She shook her head.

Damn exasperating woman. "Why ever not?"

"I didn't…"

"What?" I barked, wishing I could rein in my temper when it came to her.

"I didn't know what to do."

I let out a heavy sigh. What I should do is send her to the closest police station, but would I? Of course not. God, why did I have to be such a wanker? "Come and sit."

Before I could take her arm again, she moved out of my reach. I motioned to an empty table, pulled out her chair, and then signaled Wilder, who joined us.

"Two shots of Irish whiskey, if you would, mate," I said when Wilder got close enough to hear me. "And two more pints."

Wilder nodded and walked over to the bar.

"Start at the beginning," I said, sitting in the chair next to her.

"After you dumped me out on the street, I walked home."

"Tell me what happened when you got there." I shook my head. "And I didn't dump you in the street."

"I went into the building—"

"Where do you live?"

"Keybridge."

"Was anything out of the ordinary when you entered the lobby?"

"The doorman was nowhere to be seen, but I figured he was on break."

"There's no other security?"

"No."

"What next?"

"I took the lift to my floor and got out. I was half-way down the hall when I saw my door was ajar."

"Could it have been the landlord checking on something? Water leak maybe?"

Esland shook her head but didn't say why she was so certain it wasn't something as innocent as I was suggesting.

"I won't help you if you're unwilling to tell me the truth."

She glared at me and folded her arms, but didn't speak.

"Okay, forget the truth, then. Get on with it."

"Instead of getting back on the lift, I took the stairs."

"And?" I made a motion with my hand for her to get on with it.

"I was afraid to walk through the lobby, so I went into Café Nero."

It adjoined Keybridge; again, well done on her part. "Did anyone see you?"

"I don't think so. I stayed in the lavatory for ten minutes and then sneaked out the back door into the alley."

Everything she'd done up to that point was smart. Going into a dark alley after believing someone broke into her flat was bloody stupid.

Wilder approached and set the drinks on the table.

"Hello," he said to Esland.

"Hi," she answered in the smallest voice I'd ever heard her use.

"Be right back," I said to her and then motioned for Wilder to follow.

"Ms. Cartwright believes someone broke into her flat. Based on her demeanor, it seems she believes it's worse than that, not that she's willing to say why."

"How can I help?"

I thought it over for a minute. "Get in touch with Pique."

"Backup if I can't reach him?"

"You'll be able to; he's been out front all night. Have him take a crew over."

"Where's he going?"

"Keybridge." I walked over to Esland. "What flat number?"

"Eleven thirty-seven."

I sat down next to her after Wilder walked away. "Drink up." I pushed the shot in her direction and drank when she did.

"Thank you."

"If you're right and someone broke into your flat, you won't want to go back there tonight. Do you have anywhere you can go? Parents?"

Esland shook her head.

"What about a sister? Brother? Cousin?"

"I have no family."

She had no family? What did that mean? God, she looked so lost. "What about friends?"

She looked away again.

"I can hire a room," she whispered.

"Where?"

She shrugged.

"Right. We'll figure it out once we know more about this alleged break-in."

I waited for a snippy retort, but she remained silent.

"It may be a false alarm," I said, again trying to goad her into reacting. It was obvious she didn't think it was. However, since she was unwilling to tell me why not, there was nothing I could do but wait for Pique's report. "Come on, then," I said, standing and holding out my hand.

"Where are we going?"

"I'll introduce you." I picked up our pints and led her over to the table where my friends chatted.

The group had gathered not just to see Wren and Wilder off, but also to say goodbye to Wren's brother, Quint, who was returning to his ranch in Texas the next day.

"Everyone, this is Esland."

Quint was the first to stand and shake her hand. "Nice to meet you, miss," he drawled.

I watched as she studied him, guessing she was aware of his relationship with Darrow.

When I first met the man who had become my rival for Darrow's affections, I'd wanted to hate him. My natural reaction had been overcome by the bloke's personality. He was funny as hell, easygoing, smart, and impossible not to like.

Quint and Darrow had gotten together when she pulled her previous disappearing act and went to see Wren, who was in Texas at the time too. I should've realized then there was no hope for us to truly reconcile.

I shook my head against the hurtful memory, sat, and then pushed out the chair next to me for Esland to do the same.

"Pinch said you're friends with Darrow," said Wilder.

"That's right."

"Have we met before?"

"Yes, but it was several years ago. Dar and I were still in primary school when I last remember seeing you."

"What did you say your name was?"

"Esland Cartwright."

"Right. Yes."

When my eyes met Wilder's, I saw concern.

"My parents…"

Wilder nodded and put his hand on hers.

"Your father was Graham Cartwright," I said, suddenly realizing the connection. "He played for Willingham Allied."

When I was a lad, Wilder, Wild's older brother, Shiver, and I had gone to a WA game, probably because of Esland's friendship with Darrow. I'd had a photo taken with Graham that still sat on the bookshelf in my father's cottage. I leaned forward, close enough that only she could hear me. "I'm sorry. I never put it together."

It was coming back to me now, though. Her parents had died in a car accident on their way home from visiting their daughter at LSE—London School of Economics and Political Science.

I rested my arm on her chair and absentmindedly touched her back with my fingertips.

"You must all be very worried about Darrow," she said in an obvious attempt to change the subject.

Wren stood, walked over, and sat in the chair next to Esland. "The two of you have been friends for some time?"

I eavesdropped as Wilder's wife coaxed Esland into a conversation about her childhood and away from Darrow. The more they talked, the more I remembered the days when Wilder and I would pretend to be knights, slaying dragons on behalf of the princesses, Darrow and…God, what was it Darrow used to call her? I couldn't remember.

I was about to get another pint when I saw Pique come in the front door.

"Better if we talk outside," the man said when I approached.

"What did you find?"

"The crew is still there, gathering evidence, but it's bad, Pinch."

"Tell me."

"Not only was there a break-in, but we found a body."

"Good God."

"It gets worse." Pique handed me his mobile. I scrolled through the photos. The last one made what little hair I had stand on end.

Scrawled in blood on one of the walls were the words, "You're next, Ezzie."

"We have a forensic team there now. As I was leaving, the coroner arrived."

"Any idea who the vic is?"

"No, but I expect the coroner will determine time and cause of death as well as identity."

"Forward those photos to me."

I handed the man his mobile, and within seconds, I felt mine vibrating in receipt. "Anything else immediate I need to know?"

Pique nodded. "While it looked as though every cupboard and drawer was rummaged, we only found one destroyed item."

"What was it?"

"A photo we were able to piece together enough to see it was of a young girl with two people who looked like they could be her parents. It was ripped to shreds, most of it smeared with blood."

"Good God," I repeated, looking through the window at Esland. She raised her head and our eyes met.

"Think she did it?"

"Doubtful." I was certain she hadn't, but I couldn't say why.

"If that's the case, she needs to be in some kind of protective custody."

"Right."

"Do you want me to set it up?"

I shook my head. "I'll take care of it."

When I came inside, Esland's eyes tracked me from the door to the table.

"We're going to Sky Gardens for dinner," Wren said as I approached. "Join us?"

"Not tonight, thanks," I answered, making eye contact with Wilder, who stood and followed me over to the bar.

"Tell me."

"Dead body, death threat, and the only thing destroyed in the flat was a photo of Esland with her parents."

"What else can I do?" Wilder asked.

"I need Z to convey the investigation from the local authorities to MI5."

Alexander "Z" Archer had recently been promoted to chief of MI6, but since he'd yet to name his successor as director general of the section's domestic intelligence counterpart, he'd have to authorize MI5 taking over the investigation.

"What else, Pinch?"

"She'll need to go into protective custody."

Wilder raised a brow. "Even with the threat, she has to be questioned first."

"I'll handle it."

"Do you want Z to assign someone to her detail?"

"Like I said, I'll handle it."

"Where are you thinking of taking her? Whittaker Abbey?"

"Not with the death threat."

"It's locked down tighter than Vauxhall Cross."

The Whittaker family estate was comprised of the main residence, also known as the abbey, along with three more manor houses and several cottages. Wilder's older brother, Thornton, the current Duke of Bedfordshire, lived in the abbey with his wife and two children. And Wilder was right. Thornton, known to most as Shiver, a former high-ranking MI6 agent married to a former Russian assassin, did keep the estate locked down almost as tight as SIS headquarters.

"I'm thinking farther out."

"What about Kingham?"

I'd forgotten about the property the Whittaker family had in the Cotswolds. "Thanks, Wild. We'll leave as soon as Pique can arrange transport."

"I can make arrangements at Kingham. You needn't go."

"I'm going," I snapped.

"I see." Wilder pulled a ring of keys from his pocket, took one off, and handed it to me. "You'll receive the new security codes before your arrival."

I thanked him again and then sent a text to Pique before rejoining the group.

"What time do you leave for Texas?" I asked Quint, who stood and put his hands in his pockets.

"Nine tomorrow morning, although something tells me I should stick around a few more days."

"Appreciate it, mate, but it isn't necessary." I followed Quint's gaze to Esland.

"Whatever you need, you know that."

When I saw her pull her mobile out of her bag, I took three quick steps and snatched it from her hand.

"What are you doing?"

"What's it look like?" I powered it off and then proceeded to dismantle it.

"I need that to hire a room."

"It's taken care of."

"Where—"

"We'll discuss it later."

Before she could say anything else, I leaned down so only she could hear me. "You are either in a great deal of trouble or an equal degree of danger. Unless you'd like me to begin your questioning here and now, I suggest you keep your bloody mouth shut until we're out of the pub."

The look of fear she'd had earlier, returned, and she turned away.

"That's what I thought."

Less than two minutes later, Pique pulled up in front in a dark-colored 4x4.

"That's us," I said, taking Esland's hand and pulling her from the chair. I waved to those seated at the table and escorted her to the door, flanked by Wilder and Quint as well as three other MI5 agents who had been seated with us.

Once we reached the exit, the three agents—Grinder, Edge, and Rile—stood on either side of the doorway while Pique held the back passenger door open.

I tossed the pieces of Esland's mobile to Edge, put my arm around her, and led her outside. "Head down," I murmured. Thankfully, she complied.

When I got into the back seat after her, Edge closed the door behind us, went around to the other side, and got in the front passenger seat. By that time, Pique was behind the wheel. No sooner had Edge's door closed than Pique sped off. I glanced behind us and saw Grinder and Rile following in a similarly colored vehicle.

"It's a long drive; you can rest if you'd like," I said when I felt Esland tremble.

"What I'd like is if you'd tell me what in the bloody hell is going on."

I turned my head and looked out the window. Why had I felt compelled to protect her until she opened that bloody bee-stung mouth of hers and spoke? "Someone so unwilling to give up any information of her own should expect the same in return."

"Take me back to London," she demanded of Pique, who ignored her. She turned to me. "Where are we going?" she growled.

"Somewhere you'll be safe." I gave her the same glare and then leaned into her. "Fancy a shag last night, Esland?"

"What…are…you…talking…about?" She spat with every word.

"No male overnight guests?"

"Not that it's your business."

"In this case, it is."

"Why?"

My hand rested on my mobile. Part of me wanted to see her reaction when I showed her the image of the dead body. Another part of me decided that was going too far. My eyes met Pique's in the mirror.

"We'll discuss it later."

"We'll discuss it *now*," she demanded.

My fingers drummed on the mobile. "I didn't intend to discuss the state of your flat until we arrived at our destination. However, if you're insisting."

"I am."

I met Pique's gaze in the mirror a second time, and the man shook his head.

"You were right about your flat being broken into. It was tossed as though whoever did it was searching for something. Any idea what?"

"No." Her breathing grew heavier, and she brought her hand to her throat.

"Don't bloody lie to me, Esland," I seethed. "What were they looking for?"

"I don't know."

I tightened my grip on the mobile, so tempted to pull it out and shock her into talking. Instead, I tried one more tactic. "Is there *anything* you're willing to tell me, Ezzie?"

Her hand moved from her throat to her mouth, and she gasped. *"What did you call me?"*

"You heard me."

Once again, she turned away.

Neither of us spoke for several minutes. Finally, she turned her head back toward me. It was dark in the vehicle, but I could see she'd been crying.

"The only people who ever called me Ezzie were my parents."

"I'm sorry," I muttered.

"Why did you?"

"It was something found at your flat."

"What?"

4

Esland

"A man's dead body."

"Pull over," I shouted, covering my mouth with my hand. Thankfully, the driver did, and I made it out of the 4x4 before I lost the contents of my stomach.

Once everything was expelled, dry heaves continued to rack my insides. I felt a hand on my back and another pulling my hair away from my face. I knew it was Pinch, and as much as I didn't want him to touch me, I couldn't pull away either.

He held out a bottle of water, but I waved it away. My stomach was still trying to eliminate its contents; I couldn't add anything back in.

I kept my hands on my knees while I let Pinch's news settle in. Of everything I thought he might say, I never could've anticipated him telling me that they found a man's dead body. There was something more he hadn't told me; the dead body didn't explain why he'd referred to me as Ezzie.

"Better now?" he asked, rubbing my back.

I stood and moved out of his reach. "Tell me the rest."

Pinch handed me a handkerchief, and I wiped my mouth.

"Whatever you're involved in, someone wants you to stop."

"Are you saying I've been threatened?"

Pinch nodded.

"I recollect, not long ago, you did the same thing."

"I didn't threaten to kill you."

"Actually, you did. So, that's the threat?"

"Essentially."

If the subject we were discussing weren't so horrific, I would've grinned. Pinch just said something he hadn't intended to, and it was because I led him to do so. Score one for Esland, nine hundred and ninety-nine for Pinch.

"Whoever it was, used your nickname."

Right, because someone knew I intended to uncover the same thing that had gotten my mother and father killed. How did I explain that to Pinch without him thinking I was daft?

"We should get back on the motorway," he said.

I wiped my mouth again, put my hand on my stomach, and walked to the idling vehicle.

Even in the dark, I recognized where we were when the man driving pulled through the gate of Kingham Orchard.

"I love this place," I said as Pinch helped me out of the 4x4.

"Been here before?"

"Darrow hosted a girls' slumber here. It turned into a week-long event." Every morning, we'd walk to the farm down the road and get food to prepare for the day. Then, at night, after we ate it all, we'd go to the pub. We did that every day for a week. One day we'd even gone to a car boot sale.

I watched as he dug the key out of his pocket, opened the front door of the eighteenth-century Cotswold stone cottage, and punched a code into the entryway keypad. Once it beeped, he turned on a light, and the two men who had been with us in the 4x4 went inside, checking rooms as they went.

A few minutes later, two other men I'd met at the pub approached from the back of the house.

"How many bedrooms are there?" Pinch asked.

I wasn't sure if he was talking to me or one of the men. When no one else answered, I did. "Three."

"Show me where they are." Pinch led the way when I motioned toward the stairs.

While the exterior of the house looked as one might expect from a stone cottage, the interior had been thoroughly modernized since I'd visited. One of the three bedrooms had been transformed into a nursery, and another was an office. Every detail of the interior design of the master bedroom, as well as of the other rooms, was impeccable.

"When I was here last, those were both bedrooms," I said as we walked down the stairs and I saw one of the men bringing in a trunk I recognized as mine.

"I had them pack up some of your belongings," Pinch explained. "The rooms are upstairs," he said to the man who had been driving the 4x4 and was now carrying the trunk.

"I'll bring more provisions in the morning," he told Pinch.

"Who's staying?" Pinch asked.

"Everyone but me," the man answered.

"I'll walk you out."

5

Pinch

"Nice work," commented Pique once we were outside.

I studied the man whose sarcasm surprised me. Even though I hadn't yet been named the next director general of MI5, which I expected to be, I was still a rank above him.

"You could've handled that better."

I clenched my fist in an effort not to use it. "Are you bloody kidding me?"

"She's in danger."

I turned around and walked toward the cottage. If I didn't, I'd throttle the wanker.

"I can take over her detail if you don't want to do it. Give you time to get back to your other cases," Pique called out after me.

I spun around. "What are you about?"

"I'm just saying you don't have to stay if you don't want to."

"Explain yourself," I shouted.

"Perfectly clear if you ask me."

"What's your motive, Pique? You fancy Esland, or are you out to harm her?"

"I don't appreciate either accusation."

"Nor did I. Grinder, Rile, and Edge may answer to you, but from now on, keep in mind that I *do not*. Now, sod off and do your bloody job."

This time, no matter what came out of the man's mouth, I refused to turn around. I went inside, slamming the door behind me.

"Bugger me," I mumbled, walking into the kitchen in the hope I'd find some of my father's brandy stored in the cupboard.

"Everything okay?"

I was rarely caught unaware, but I hadn't seen Esland sitting at the table.

"It's fine."

"Right."

I almost cheered when I found not one, but two of the unmarked bottles.

"What's that?" she asked when I poured a glass.

"We call it Wellie's brandy. Want some?"

"Definitely. How is your father? I heard he was ill."

"He's much better now. Thank you."

"He's always kept such good care of the grounds."

My father and grandfather before him were the head groundskeepers at the abbey. As a child, the three Whittaker siblings and I had explored every nook and cranny of the vast estate. While my father lived in a modest cottage rather than in the abbey itself or in one of the other manor houses, I'd always considered the estate my home in the same way the Whittakers did.

"I thought that's where you were taking me."

"No." I didn't tell her about Wilder's offer, or that I preferred being farther away from London.

"You understand that your life was threatened, Esland?"

She looked out the window even though it was too dark to see anything.

"You're not surprised."

"I'm a journalist. Many of us are threatened or even killed for the injustices we expose."

"This is personal. Whoever is issuing the threat knows you as Ezzie."

She wouldn't look at me, which was to be expected. Her hand went to her throat, indicating her subconscious was in protective mode.

"There will be an investigation into the murder. MI5 will take over and can keep it out of the media. However, if there's anything I need to know before we're involved in an official capacity, this is your opportunity to tell me."

"Are you going back to London tonight?"

"I'm not going anywhere."

That surprised her enough that she turned and looked at me. "Tomorrow?"

I shook my head. "You are, for all intents and purposes, under protective custody."

"I'm in custody?"

"Listen to what I say, Esland. Under, not in. It means I'm keeping you safe."

"There must be others who could do that."

Right. There were presently three others on Kingham grounds who could very well do the job. However, until I was able to gain clarity on why my gut was insisting I be the one to protect her, I'd listen to instinct alone.

"You don't even like me."

True statement, although it was more the job she did and how it impacted my investigations that I didn't care for.

"Why did you say you were at the pub to see me earlier?" I asked. "Were you already aware of the dead man in your flat?"

"No."

"So why?"

She shrugged.

"You're not a child, Esland. I'll ask again. Why were you at the pub to see me?"

"I wanted to talk to you about Darrow. And then you dumped me in the street. Nice move, by the way."

"First, sarcasm has no place in our conversations. Second, you're lying to me. Lastly, as I said before, I didn't dump you anywhere."

"Why did you do it?" she asked. "Am I really that horrible of a person, or that much of a nuisance?"

I honestly couldn't tell her why I'd picked her up and carried her out of the pub. Even I had to admit it was a wanker's move.

"I'm sorry I did that."

"Are you refusing to answer my question?"

"To be honest with you, I don't know why."

I saw a slight nod of understanding.

"Thank you for the apology."

She did rub on my nerves, but was it her job or was it something else entirely? When Pique offered to take over Esland's detail, my reaction had been inexplicable as well. I'd immediately felt an overwhelming need to protect her, even from my colleague. When she asked if I was returning to London, a feeling settled in my chest like a heavy stone. The idea of entrusting her safety to anyone else was unacceptable. *Why?* I couldn't explain it.

"Tell me about your parents."

She sighed, taking a long time to answer. "I miss them so much."

"I'm sure you do. What were they like?"

"I never doubted they loved me."

"But?"

"They were a unit unto themselves. I was the third to two who didn't need one."

I didn't hear hurt in her voice; I heard acceptance.

"They were on their way home from visiting you when the accident happened."

"Yes. I was at university."

"Must've been rough. You said earlier that you have no other family."

"Both my parents were only children. I don't think they ever tried to have another child."

So no aunts, uncles, or cousins, also like she'd said earlier.

"Why journalism?"

"My mother was a reporter, albeit a very different one than I am."

"How so?"

"She was more of a social reporter."

"How would you describe yourself?"

"Investigative."

"As I well know."

When I saw a slight smile from her, I smiled too.

"I never told a soul about Wren's true identity."

I nodded.

"I told you earlier that I found out from Darrow."

"Yes." I shook my head. One would've thought Darrow, of all people, would've known better.

Esland stood. "Where am I sleeping?"

"Bedroom."

"I can sleep on a sofa somewhere. I don't need to take the only bed."

"Not up for discussion."

"You're very intransigent, aren't you? Your way or no way?"

"Sometimes."

"Right. Only sometimes. I wonder if Darrow would agree?"

I watched Esland walk away, knowing her estimation was dead-on. Darrow would say that I consistently refused to compromise, that I wouldn't apologize, or even try to see things her way. I could hear her voice in my head, saying all of those things. Not that she was any less stubborn than I was.

Edge pulled out a chair and joined me a few minutes after Esland went upstairs. "What are our orders?"

"Standard protection. Figure out a schedule and rotate through positions."

"Understood."

"Any idea what's up Pique's arse?" I probably shouldn't put Edge on the spot, but as the boss, I needed an answer.

"I don't know, but if I had to guess, Miss Cartwright is…attractive."

"Beyond unprofessional."

"Agreed." Edge shrugged. "So, when are you returning to London?"

"I haven't decided." I was lying, but the real answer was as open-ended.

I sent Pique a text asking him to swing by MI5 headquarters and pick up a bag I kept in my office in the event I had to leave at a moment's notice.

After Pique responded, I went upstairs. There was a sofa in the room that had been set up as an office. Sleeping there would put me on the wall opposite of where Esland slept. *Sleeping*—as if I'd be doing much of that.

6

Esland

I sat down on the bed and hugged the pillow. What in God's name had I gotten myself mixed up in? Had I been the intended victim today, but instead, some other bloke was offed in my place? Who the hell was he anyway? I was afraid I knew the answer.

That murder, combined with the death threat against me, in which someone had used the nickname no one other than my parents ever did, sent the adrenaline of terror coursing through my veins.

I groaned aloud, pulling the hair my fingers were twisted in. What…the…fuck was I going to do? Contact the man who got me mixed up in this in the first place—if he was still alive? He'd explicitly told me not to, saying that when he knew more, I would too.

I wished I could rewind the clock seventy-two hours and not even take the man's call. Agreeing to meet him was what had set this horrifying train in motion.

But what choice had I had? When he began the conversation, he'd said he had something to tell me about my parents. Then when we'd met two days ago, he let me know he had information that suggested their death wasn't the accident it had been ruled as.

And Pinch? What in God's name had I been thinking, going to him?

Darrow had made the suggestion. The same night she told me about Wren's true identity, she'd told me that if I ever found myself in trouble—serious trouble—I should go to Pinch and he'd help me. Darrow promised I could trust him regardless of what was involved. It was as though Darrow had had a premonition of what was coming.

After my meeting with the former footballer, I'd tried to contact Darrow, only to find out she'd gone missing. That was when I'd known I had no choice but to go to Pinch.

I'd stalked him and then followed him into the pub, but before I had a chance to tell him why I was there, he summarily tossed me on the street. I had to admit it was my fault. Instead of telling him I needed his help, I got distracted when I realized Wren Whittaker was there too.

After seeing the door to my flat ajar, though, I knew I had no choice but to go back and beg him to listen to me. From there, my nightmare had escalated into something so much worse.

Still, knowing he was here with me, that he intended to stay, took some of my fear away. There was something about him that made me believe I could trust him, even after he'd threatened me over Wren.

I informed him I hadn't told a soul about the agent's true identity, but I hadn't said why I didn't take the story to the *Times*.

The bottom line was, Wren and I weren't so different. We both acted on a fundamental belief that there was a difference between right and wrong, and wrong could not be ignored—no matter the personal cost. Somehow, I knew Pinch would understand that, if I could only bring myself to confide in him.

For the second time, I groaned out loud. Ever since Darrow had suggested I could trust him if I was ever in trouble, I found myself fantasizing about him, and that made me the worst friend in the history of friendships.

If I could ask, would Darrow say she and Pinch were finished? Or would she say she was still in love with him?

What about Wren's brother, Quint? The last time Darrow had pulled a disappearing act, she ended up involved with him even though initially she'd only gone to visit Wren.

Where was she now? Did she flee to the sanctuary of yet another friend? Did that friend have a brother too?

The bottom line was I had no business thinking about Darrow's ex-boyfriend in the context I almost always did. In my fantasies, it didn't matter that he couldn't abide me in real life. No, when I closed my eyes and let myself think about him, he abided me just fine.

"Esland?" The knock on the bedroom door startled me.

"Yes?" I responded, but didn't get up.

"Everything okay?"

"Yes," I said a second time, hugging my knees to my chest.

"Are you sure?" Pinch asked.

Why was he asking? I stood and opened the door. "Has something else happened?"

"No. Just checking on you."

I rested my head against the door. "I'm sorry I was such a bitch earlier."

He cocked his head.

"It's just…everything that's happened…"

He looked beyond me into the room. "Did I wake you?"

"No. I don't sleep much."

"Me either."

"Was there anything else?" I looked into his eyes, wishing he would push past me, stretch out on the bed, and hold me in his arms until I fell asleep. I shook my head at the ridiculousness of the fantasy.

"What?" he asked, his voice so soft I hardly heard him.

"Nothing."

"It's something." He put his hand above my head, gripping the door. His eyes, green in the dim light, bored into mine. "I'm sorry about what I did earlier at the pub. It was a wanker move."

"I'm not going to say it was okay, but you did warn me. Plus, you already apologized."

Pinch smiled. "I'm glad you trusted me enough, in spite of it, to come back and ask for my help."

"I do trust you, Pinch. You may be the only person I can."

His hand that gripped the door slid down, and he brushed my hair from my face. "We'll talk more tomorrow."

"Will you still be here?"

"I told you before I would be."

"Why?" I blurted before I could stop myself.

Pinch touched my cheek with his fingertips. "I don't know," he answered, walking away, but stopping before going into the room next door. "I'm right here if you need me."

"Thanks," I whispered and closed my door. If he only knew how much I did.

I unzipped my skirt, let it fall to the floor, and then unbuttoned my blouse and draped it over the chair next to the bed. I unfastened my bra and let it slide off my shoulders. While I normally slept in the nude, I thought better of it with Pinch next door. Not that he'd be back.

I opened the trunk, thankful when I saw that whoever had packed it, included a T-shirt. After putting it on, I crawled under the covers and hugged the same pillow I had earlier, wishing I had something to read to help take my mind off what was happening so I could sleep.

Remembering there were bookcases in the main level drawing room, I crawled out of bed and eased the door open so I wouldn't disturb Pinch. I crept down the stairs, relieved when I didn't hear any sound coming from his room.

When I rounded the corner, I knew why; Pinch was standing in front of the same bookcases I was headed to. Before I could go upstairs unnoticed, he turned around, looking from my face down to where my T-shirt skimmed the middle of my thighs, and back to my face.

"I was going to look for a book."

Pinch shut the one he was thumbing through and motioned with his hand for me to go ahead.

"I can come back later." I'd just reached the banister when I felt Pinch's hand on my shoulder.

"You don't need to leave."

I took a deep breath, turned around, and looked into his piercing eyes. "I'm sorry."

"What are you sorry for?"

"Everything." I attempted to escape upstairs a second time.

"Esland," he said, grasping my hand and pulling me into the drawing room with him.

"Pinch, I—"

"My name is Axel."

"Right. Well, I—"

"Say it."

Why, instead of being affronted by his growly tone, did my barely covered panties moisten? "Say what?"

"My name."

His hand slid to my waist. He pulled my body flush with his, and his lips touched the skin below my ear. "Say my name," he repeated. "Like you used to."

"Axel."

7

Pinch

With my right arm around her waist, I reached up and cupped Esland's cheek with my left hand.

I was within a fraction of an inch from kissing her when I heard her whisper, "We can't."

Instead, I rested my forehead against hers. I wanted to ask why we couldn't, not because I didn't know, but because there were so many reasons.

Foremost, she was vulnerable and under my protection. I'd also made it clear on several occasions, including a few short hours ago, that I found her annoying.

"You don't like me," I heard her say as though she'd read my mind.

When she tried to turn away from me, I tightened my grasp. "You're wrong."

"I drive you crazy."

"That, you're right about, but not in the way you mean it."

"Darrow."

"Darrow and I are no longer together."

This time when Esland wriggled away, I let her go.

"I'm sorry, Pinch—I just can't." She ran up the stairs. Seconds later, I heard the bedroom door close.

I'd known that was her primary reason for stopping the kiss, but it was no longer relevant; Darrow and I were finished. We had been since shortly after she returned from the States at Thanksgiving.

Our brief reconciliation and subsequent breakup had culminated with Darrow inviting Quint to Whittaker Abbey for Christmas. Even if she hadn't, we wouldn't have gotten back together.

But as far as Esland was concerned, setting the issue of any past relationships aside, I was a person in a position of trust who had just made an inappropriate move on someone under my protection. She was vulnerable, and I'd exploited her fragile state.

I knew all of this, and yet more than anything, I wanted to follow her up the stairs, take her in my arms, and kiss her breathless. Why, though? My reaction to her was so unlike me.

I let out a deep breath, knowing what I had to do. Tomorrow, I'd find someone to take my place, and then I'd return to London. I pulled my mobile out and then put it away again. Who would I call? Who could I trust to watch over Esland? To keep her safe?

The most troubling question was the one I couldn't answer: why did it matter so much to me?

It was close to three in the morning by the time I finally went upstairs. I'd dozed off on the sofa in the drawing room several times, but never for more than five or ten minutes.

I'd had two conversations each with Edge, Grinder, and Rile and hadn't asked any of them to take over Esland's detail for me. Not even Rile, who was officially MI6 but had offered to help when he heard what had happened.

I heard a noise on the other side of the wall and woke with a start. The bedroom door opened and closed, followed by the bathroom door doing the same.

I checked the time; it was half past seven. I wasn't surprised Esland was up this early; I only hoped she got more sleep than I had.

I sat up on the sofa, attempted to stretch my cramped muscles, and grabbed my trousers. I hoped like hell Pique would arrive with my bag sometime this morning. But did it matter? Shouldn't I leave today anyway?

I stood, shaking my head before pulling my undershirt over it.

A few seconds later, I heard the creak of the bathroom door followed by Esland's footfalls on the floor of the hallway. I didn't bother to don my dress shirt or my shoes, although halfway down the stairs, I thought maybe I should've. What if she went out the front door? I'd have to call one of the guys to go after her.

She didn't. She was in the kitchen, filling the kettle.

When I said good morning, she dropped it in the sink.

"I'm sorry I startled you."

"It's okay. Good morning," she said without looking at me.

I walked over and stood next to her. "We have a lot to talk about today."

She stared at the water coming from the faucet.

"To begin, I want to apologize for last night. I was out of line."

Esland turned away and set the kettle on the stove. "It's okay," she said a second time.

"It isn't."

She stood with one foot on top of the other, still not looking at me. "I suppose someone needs to question me about the man found in my flat."

"Do you think you'd be up for looking at a photo to see if he was someone you knew?"

Her hand went to her stomach. "Sure." She turned the fire off on the stove.

"You can still make tea."

"I won't be able to drink it, so there's hardly a point."

"We don't have to do anything right this minute."

"The idea of it is bad enough on its own." She walked out of the kitchen and into the drawing room.

"Esland?" I followed her. "We don't have to do this at all."

"You have photos? I want to see them."

Once again, I felt like kicking myself. Why hadn't I edited them when I had the chance? She didn't need to see them all, but if I handed her my mobile, she'd certainly scroll through them.

The same mobile containing the photos vibrated in my hand.

"Pinch," I answered.

"It's Z."

"Yes, Z."

"Bring me up to speed."

I excused myself and went upstairs. "What do you already know?"

"Everything up to the point when you made the decision to take a murder suspect out of the immediate jurisdiction, demanded that MI5 take the case over from the local police, and then crowned yourself the suspect's protector when you already have a full caseload."

By the time Z got to the end of his rant, he was shouting.

"Am I still being considered for the DG spot?" I asked.

"For God's sake, what's this about?"

"Answer the question."

"Sod off, Pinch. You know you are."

"Then, I would think you would know that I know what I'm doing."

"Very well. Explain."

Bugger. Of course Z would ask me to, and I couldn't. There was nothing rational or logical about me bringing Esland here or assigning myself to her detail when it was something any of the three men on premise could handle without me.

"I was about to begin questioning Ms. Cartwright when you rang."

"Do you think she murdered the bloke?"

"I don't."

"Any other suspects?"

"All I've learned thus far is that whoever broke into her flat, tossed it, obviously looking for something. Also, it's close to home, given no one has ever called her Ezzie other than her parents."

"Surely, someone knew they did. She was in her twenties when they died."

"Not by her reaction when I used the name."

"What does she think they were looking for?"

I half laughed. "You don't think I would've led with that if she'd said?"

"The rest of your brain seems brandy-addled. I thought you may have forgotten."

"I'm hoping she'll confide in me this morning. She did come to me for help, after all."

"Right. When will you be back in the office?"

"I don't know."

Z ended the call without another word, but none were necessary. As I'd pointed out, I knew what I was doing. Actually, I didn't, except for the part about not having any choice but to stick with what my gut was telling me.

I grabbed my shoes and went downstairs. Esland was still standing where she'd been when I went up to take Z's call.

"Are you ready?" she asked.

"To show you the photos?"

Esland nodded.

"No. I've decided against it."

Esland rolled her eyes. *Rolled her eyes.* "My flat. Threat on my life. Hand them over."

"It's bad, Esland."

"Who exactly do you think I am?"

That question threw me. "What do you mean?"

"I'm a bloody investigative reporter. I'm in the trenches. I see things every day that no one should see. You don't think I've seen dead people?"

"Have you seen one in your own flat?"

"You know I haven't."

"Most people wouldn't jump to the conclusion that their flat was broken into just because they found the door open. Most people don't accept a death threat like yesterday's news."

"I was hardly unaffected by it."

She was chewing her thumbnail, something I'd noticed before that she did when she was…what? Nervous? Frightened? I walked over and wrapped my fingers around her wrist. When she tried to yank her hand away, I held on tighter.

"Pique had to pull the 4x4 to the side of the road if I remember correctly."

"Interesting name. It was good of you to introduce us."

"Sarcasm—"

"Has no business in our conversation."

I smiled when she repeated what I'd said to her yesterday. "Is a childish way to avoid telling the truth."

"Sod off," she said, this time getting me to release my hold on her.

I sat in a chair and leaned forward with my elbows on my knees. "Don't bite your nails."

"Don't tell me what to do." Her response was knee-jerk, and by the flush on her cheeks, I knew she wished she hadn't reacted that way.

"You must trust me, or you wouldn't have come to me."

"In certain matters, yes."

That stung a bit, but I'd get over it. "What were they looking for?"

"I already said that I don't know."

"Tell me the truth, Ezzie." I used the name intentionally to provoke her, but it didn't seem to faze her in the slightest until she turned her back on me.

"Don't do that."

"Call you Ezzie?"

"You don't mean it."

I didn't need to ask what she meant. Her parents had used the name as a term of endearment. I stood and walked over to her, putting my hands on her shoulders. "And if I do?"

"Pinch—"

"Axel."

Instead of trying to get away from me as I expected her to do, Esland leaned back and rested her head on my chest.

"Where the fuck is Darrow?" she whispered.

I laughed. Once again, she surprised me. Not many did, yet she seemed to do it with regularity.

"I've told you that's finished."

"You know how she is."

I nodded. I knew Darrow Whittaker better than anyone, and yet, I wouldn't be able to predict her reaction if Esland asked about the status of our relationship.

"Do you think something's happened to her?"

"I don't."

"Why?"

"I just don't."

"Does her family share your ambivalence?"

"You mistake my inability to discuss her whereabouts with a *Times* reporter for something that it definitely is not."

She turned around and looked into my eyes. "You know where she is, don't you?"

While lying was a regular part of my job, I found that in this instance, I couldn't lie to Esland. "I do."

"How can you let everyone worry—"

"Wilder and Wren left on their honeymoon because they know too. Quint returned to Texas for the same reason."

"Does everyone in the family know?"

"Need-to-know basis, but yes."

"I see. So, there's no reason for worry?"

"None whatsoever."

She shrugged away from me and sat on the sofa. "Back to the photos."

"I'm not showing them to you. I told you before that I changed my mind."

"Just show me the body."

8

Esland

Pinch hesitated but pulled his mobile out and swiped the screen. He sat down and held it for me to see.

The man had been beaten so badly I wouldn't have known who he was, save for the one thing on his hand that identified him. The man wore the same 2010 Master League Football Championship ring my father had. His hands had swollen over the years, as his body had, with excess weight, and it no longer fit on his ring finger, so he wore it on his right pinky.

"You know him?" asked Pinch, moving the mobile out of my line of vision.

"It's Tommy Sholes."

"No doubt in your mind?"

"None whatsoever."

"He played for Willingham Allied at the same time your father did."

"Look at his right hand."

Pinch swiped the screen once more. "I can't make out anything."

If I hadn't known what it was from noticing it when I met him the other day, I wouldn't have been able to make it out either. "Look," I said, putting my finger right where the ring was in the photo.

"You aren't surprised by who it is."

"No."

Pinch stood and walked over to the window where we'd been standing moments before. When he rubbed the back of his neck with his hand, it was as though I could see him processing the information I'd just shared with him.

"Whatever you know, he knew too."

"Was the other way around."

"He was severely beaten before they put a bullet in his brain. What information were they trying to get out of him?"

"I don't know."

I watched as Pinch continued processing. "You just said that you knew what he knew."

I shook my head. "He didn't get the chance to tell me."

"But you met with him?"

I nodded.

"When?"

"Day before yesterday."

"What did you discuss?"

I hesitated. Saying it out loud was harder than I'd imagined it would be. I took a deep breath, unsuccessfully willing my eyes not to fill with tears. I looked away. "My parents' death wasn't an accident."

"Was that all?"

"No."

"Esland, please."

"He said that my father would've wanted me to finish what he started."

"What does that mean?"

I shrugged. "I'm telling you the truth, Pinch. I don't know."

"You're a reporter. You must have a theory."

"The only other thing Tommy said was that what my father knew, had something to do with the Master League."

"You didn't ask what he meant?"

I didn't care for his tone one bit. This was already hard enough on me.

"Sod off, Pinch." I turned to walk away, but he grabbed my arm.

"I'm trying to help you."

"Of course I asked what it bloody well meant. What do you take me for?"

When he spoke again, his voice was measured. "What was his response?"

"That he'd never been able to figure out what it was either."

"Why did he come to you now?"

My eyes filled with tears a second time. "He was dying."

Pinch scrubbed his face. "Whoever killed him, knew that you and Tommy met."

"Yes."

"You knew you were in danger when you first came looking for me."

"Yes."

"What else did you and Sholes discuss?"

"He said that when he knew more, I would too. He told me not to do anything until he talked to someone else he believed could help us."

"Sholes didn't divulge who that was?"

"Of course not." My eyes filled with tears *again*. "Now he's dead and it's my fault."

Pinch wrapped his arm around my shoulders and pulled me close to him. "It isn't."

My tears turned into sobs as I let myself really cry for the first time since I'd initially been approached by the man who was now dead.

"Let it out," he whispered, stroking my hair with one hand while he tightened his hold on me with the other.

The relief I felt over telling Pinch as much as I had was palpable.

"You must've been so frightened," he murmured.

His words surprised me. I'd believed Pinch to be hardened, impatient, by-the-book, and even intolerant. Instead, he cut straight to the heart of what I was feeling.

I startled when I heard the front door open and tried to move away from him, but Pinch held me tighter. I heard someone clear his throat.

"Wait outside," Pinch said without looking to see who it was.

The man didn't respond, but I heard the front door open and close.

"Do you know who that was?"

"Pique."

"You knew just by him clearing his throat?"

"I knew because if it had been Edge, Grinder, or Rile, they would've turned around and walked out without my needing to tell them to."

"But not Pique?"

"No."

"Why not?"

"I don't know, but I intend to find out."

I shifted so I was no longer leaning against him. "Thank you."

"I'm afraid to ask what for," he said with a glint in his eyes that, today, were a piercing shade of blue.

"For being so nice to me."

"I knew you were going to say that. Darrow must've led you to believe I was quite the wanker."

"She never said a word against you."

"Surprising, but okay."

"Let's just say that before yesterday, you weren't always…nice. In fact, you never were."

Rather than say it was because I was a reporter who annoyed him on the regular, Pinch apologized.

"I'm sorry I've been such a pest," I responded.

"Just doing your job." He smiled.

"As were you."

"Since we've established a mutual fan club, I suppose I should see what Pique has to report."

"Will you tell him?"

"What you've told me? No. Not yet."

"Why not?"

"I don't know, but I intend to find out," he repeated.

"That makes no sense."

"Sure, it does," he said, leaning down to brush my forehead with his lips before he stood and walked toward the front door.

When I heard it close behind him and I was certain he was gone, I leaned against the back of the sofa.

The man who had the starring role in my fantasies had just kissed me, albeit on my forehead. Not only that, he'd listened; he'd reassured me; he did all the things I dreamed he'd do, not believing he would in reality.

However, when I closed my eyes, it wasn't Pinch's face I saw. It wasn't Tommy's either—it was Darrow's.

9

Pinch

"Sorry for interrupting."

I didn't respond.

"The coroner has an ID on the vic. He's Thomas Sholes, former center midfielder for Willingham Allied. Cause of death was blunt force trauma. Not sure why they shot him."

"To send a message."

"To Esland?"

"Of course to Esland."

Pique shifted on his feet. "Listen, I put my foot in it yesterday. I had no right to question your tactics or suggest I knew how to handle the situation better than you."

"Why did you?"

Pique looked off in the distance. "It was completely unprofessional on my part."

"Agreed. Now answer my question."

He cleared his throat like he had earlier. "There's just something about her that makes a man want to protect her."

I agreed, although I didn't intend to say so.

"Are you…"

I raised a brow.

"Sorry. Not my business."

"Where's my satchel?"

"Bugger me," Pique responded, shifting his feet again. "I'm sorry, Pinch. Completely forgot once I got off the phone with the coroner. I'll head back to London and retrieve it."

I shook my head. "I'll have Z bring it."

"I didn't realize he was on his way."

"He isn't…yet."

"What would you like me to do?"

"Follow up with forensics. See if there is any evidence whatsoever to be had."

"Right."

I turned to go inside.

"Are we resolved?" Pique asked.

"For now."

I didn't see Esland when I went inside, but I heard noises from upstairs. I found her in the master bedroom, rummaging through her trunk.

"Everything okay?" I asked.

"I was hoping someone has packed my tablet."

"I wouldn't allow you to use it anyway."

"I noticed my laptop disappeared."

"Once we know it isn't being tracked, you can have it back. However—"

Esland held up her hand. "I get it, Pinch."

I walked closer. "I wish you'd call me Axel."

She stood straight up and put one hand on her hip. "Why? You don't like Pinch? Everyone calls you that."

"I didn't say I wanted everyone to use my given name. I said I want you to."

"Interesting," she said, dropping her hand.

"What's that?"

"You don't want me to use your nickname, or whatever you call it, and yet, you won't stop using mine."

"I'm going to have to bring Z in on this," I said, changing the subject.

"Whatever you think is best."

I stared into her eyes. God, I wanted to kiss her. More than I'd wanted to kiss any other woman, and that included Darrow.

I heard someone coming up the stairs and took a step back.

"Sorry, Pinch," said Edge, standing in the doorway. "George is trying to reach you."

"Right. Thanks," I responded and turned to Esland. "I need to return this call."

"Can I go outside?"

I cocked my head. "Of course."

"I wasn't sure…you know…"

I smiled. "Even the airspace here is covered."

Her eyes opened wide. "Really?"

"No, but you're safe. Edge won't be far away." The man was standing at the top of the staircase and nodded to both Esland and me when we walked out of the room.

"Hello, Pinch," said George when she answered my call. "Z tells me you've gone off your trolley."

"Don't count on it."

Leighton "George" Marietta was my sole competition for the director general position at MI5. She was an outstanding agent, equally qualified for the job, and honestly, if Z went with her over me, I would understand. That didn't mean I intended to hand it to her, though.

"We'll be there by early afternoon. Anything you need us to bring?"

"My satchel."

"Done. Anything else?"

"Whatever reports have come in thus far."

"I understand the coroner was able to identify the victim," she said.

"Tommy Sholes."

"Right. Willingham Allied star."

"Once was."

"Played with Graham Cartwright," she added.

"That's right."

"I remember the accident. All of the UK went into mourning."

"His daughter has reason to believe it wasn't an accident."

"At the time, I didn't think it was, either, Pinch."

Interesting. I couldn't wait to hear why, once she and Z arrived.

I disconnected the call, stuffed my mobile in my back pocket, and went downstairs in search of Esland.

10

Esland

It was too chilly for a walk, but I needed the fresh air to catch my breath and attempt to clear my mind.

What in the name of God had happened in the last hour? One minute Pinch and I were arguing about his refusal to show me photos of who I now knew was Tommy Sholes, and the next, he'd looked as though he wanted to kiss me.

I stopped under a tree and covered my face with my hands. I had to be losing my mind. There was no other explanation for it.

When I'd run away from his kiss last night, I was steadfast in knowing I was doing the right thing. I owed Darrow that much, without, at the very minimum, talking to her about it. Since Darrow was evidently unreachable at the moment, I had no intention of coming within arm's reach of Pinch again. But, God, I wanted to know how his lips would feel, his tongue dancing with mine, his naked body beside me.

"Good God," I groaned. It wasn't as though I was still a girl in secondary school. I was a grown woman—an adult—who knew better than to poach my best friend's man.

I heard the front door close and saw the man himself walking toward me. It was a sight I could linger over for hours.

I wondered if he'd ever played football; he was certainly athletic-enough looking to have. His physique lent itself to him being a target man, but that wasn't all that made my mouth water. His self-assurance added exponentially to his allure. And those eyes. I could get lost in them for days.

"You look as though you're fixing to eat me alive, Ezzie."

I felt my cheeks flush. "In a manner of speaking."

The last thing anyone would accuse me of, would be a prude. In fact, it was quite the opposite. Among my group of friends at university, raunchy jokes were known to be my forte. However, when I was around Pinch, I found myself blushing as much as a twenty-nine-year-old virgin. Which I wasn't. What was it about him that made me want to *behave*? I shuddered at the word.

"Esland?"

I rolled my shoulders. "Um, did you reach Z or George or whomever was trying to reach you?"

"I did, and they're on their way here. Do you want to tell me what else is going on with you?"

"Let's see…Someone was killed in my flat. Someone who believed my parents' death was no accident. On top of that, whoever killed him threatened to kill me too. I'm in the bloody Cotswolds where I have to ask permission to go outside, and if all of that isn't bad enough, I spent the morning wishing I could kiss my best friend's boyfriend."

My admission didn't seem to faze him. "I'm not her boyfriend. Darrow and I are finished."

"Right. Until the next time she shows up from God knows where she is and curls her finger in your direction."

"No." He shook his head. "Not happening."

My heart wanted to believe him, but my brain knew better.

"When do your colleagues arrive?"

"Early this afternoon."

I walked past him toward the cottage, not bothering to see if he followed. I needed time alone without him assaulting each of my senses.

Once inside, I went upstairs to the bedroom and looked through the clothes someone had packed for me. The idea of it—that someone had gone into my flat, rummaged through my bureau drawers and wardrobe—made me physically sick to my stomach.

I flexed my fingers, achy with the need to write. Since I'd learned to do so, it was how I processed my feelings. I started my first diary before I began primary school. I still had all of them too. The first was barely legible, full of sometimes-indecipherable misspellings, yet what jumped off the page were my feelings.

If only I'd been able to ask the agent who packed my clothes to bring it for me.

My eyes flew open, and my hand went to my throat. I ran from the room and downstairs in search of Pinch.

"My bloody diary," I shouted when I found him talking to Edge.

When I got close enough, Pinch put his hands on my shoulders. "What was in it?"

"Everything Tommy said to me."

"When you say 'everything,' what does that mean?"

"That he said my father would want me to finish what he'd started."

"Anything else?"

I nodded.

"You can trust me," he murmured.

"I wrote that I planned to go to you." God, what had I done? I'd just put him in as much danger as I was in. Whoever killed Sholes wouldn't just be looking for me, they'd be looking for Pinch too.

"I know what you're thinking. Whether they found your diary or not, they know you're with me now. They may not know where, but they know."

"How could they not know where?"

"Trust me, Esland." Pinch had his mobile out and was calling someone.

"I'll go back inside."

He moved his hand from my shoulder to the back of my neck. "Pique," he said into the mobile. "I need you to check something for me. There was a diary." Pinch held the phone away from his ear so I could hear the man's response.

"I don't recall seeing one."

Pinch covered the mic with his hand. "Where was it?"

"Ask him if the bed was tossed."

"I can answer that. It didn't appear to be."

"You could tell from the photos?"

Pinch nodded. "Thanks, Pique."

He ended the call before I heard whether Pique responded.

"I'll have George retrieve it. She can be trusted not to look at its contents if she's able to find it."

"George is a woman?"

"Yes," he answered simply.

"Why are you having my diary retrieved?"

"Because it's yours, and no one else should know its contents."

"But wouldn't it be evidence?"

"There's enough evidence without it."

"I doubt your George will agree, or Z for that matter."

"Not *my* George, and if she doesn't agree, Z will know to do as I ask."

When I felt Pinch's fingers massaging the back of my neck, I twisted out of his grasp.

"Why do you continue to pull away from me?"

I laughed. "You aren't daft, Pinch. Don't act as though you are."

"Pretend I am."

"One word. *Darrow.*" I walked away, and for the second time that morning, he didn't follow.

11

Pinch

I knew what I had to do. I needed Esland to trust me enough to confide in me so I could figure out who was after her and why. In order for that to happen, I needed Darrow in an entirely different way than I had in the past.

Instead of waiting for her to come back to me, this time I needed her to let me go. That part wasn't as difficult to imagine as the part that came after. How would Darrow feel when she read between the lines and saw I was interested in Esland? I wouldn't be able to hide it from her; she'd see right through it. More than how she'd feel, how would she react? There was simply no telling.

Two hours later, I arrived in Portsmouth and was motioned through the gate without having to show my identification. I pulled up to the main building and saw JohnTwo, as they'd referred to now-General Carleton Pope back when he was my training officer.

"I was surprised to hear from you so early in the Duchess of Monckton's training."

I laughed. "That bad, is she?"

"Hardly. Just an easy mark. Better than Princess, right?"

"How's she doing, really?"

"Fine," answered Pope. "Better than. She's lived your life as well as her brothers' long enough that some of what she's learning is innate."

"I'm sorry to pull her away, but I'm afraid it's unavoidable."

"No better training than a real-life investigation, I say."

"I don't intend to keep her away long. Twenty-four hours, forty-eight at the most."

Pope nodded and then pointed toward the transport vehicle carrying who I could already tell was a very pissed off Darrow.

"What the bloody hell, Axel?" she said once Pope left us alone.

"I understand that you and Esland Cartwright are close friends. She's in trouble." I watched as Darrow's ire receded.

"What's happened?"

"A man was found dead in her flat. Whoever killed him, left a message for her, saying she was next."

Darrow covered her mouth with her hand. "Oh, God. Poor True."

True. That's what Darrow used to call Esland. Later, I'd ask why. Now we needed to get on the road.

"I need your help, Darrow."

"Of course. What can I do?"

"Help convince her to trust me."

"I don't understand."

"I'll explain on the way."

"Wait. I'm leaving?"

"I'll have you back as quickly as I can."

12

Esland

"What do you mean he isn't here?" I heard a woman say.

"He left shortly after I told him to ring you."

I wouldn't know who was speaking if I hadn't heard Edge tell Pinch to call George earlier.

"I don't understand. Did he say where he was going?"

Edge didn't respond. I guessed he probably shook his head.

"Is Ms. Cartwright here?"

Again, no verbal response.

Rather than continuing to eavesdrop, I went downstairs. Halfway there, I immediately recognized the woman who must be George. I also recognized the salt-and-pepper gray-haired man standing behind her. I'd seen the two of them together once.

When my eyes met the woman's, I knew George recognized me too. Especially when her cheeks pinkened.

If the circumstances of why I was at Kingham Cross weren't so dire, I'd be tempted to shout out that the two of them were busted. The idea of it made me smile. It was official—I was losing my bloody mind.

"Where is Agent Fulton?" the woman asked, but she must've realized she'd forgotten her manners because she added, "I'm Agent Marietta, and this is Chief Alexander from MI6."

"Z and George, right?" I said, stepping forward to shake both of their hands. "And to answer your question, I have no idea where Agent Fulton has run off to. Perhaps he's gone by the same way as Darrow Whittaker."

Inside my head, I was laughing maniacally. Perhaps the stress of my situation had put me in shock, or I was mad as a hatter. That seemed more likely.

But seriously, where the fuck was Pinch? He'd left because I refused to kiss him? He'd been right yesterday when he said he was a wanker.

"Straight to voicemail," said Z, dropping the hand holding his mobile from his ear and leveling a serious gaze at me. Well, he could fuck off too. No one asked MI6 to get involved. MI5 either.

That wasn't true. I'd gone to Pinch. They could be mad at me for that if they wanted to. Frankly, they could both right sod off. If they wanted to leave me on my own, I'd figure my way somehow. Maybe I should go to the *Times,* or the peelers' station near Keybridge.

"Pinch asked me to bring this to you," said George, handing me a clear plastic bag containing my diary.

"Thanks," I said, clutching it to my chest and praying no one in the room had read it. Not only had I written about my meeting with Tommy Sholes, but it was full of silly ramblings about a certain agent who, it seemed, had disappeared like his former girlfriend had.

"See if Rile, Grinder, or Pique know where Pinch is," Z said to Edge, who nodded and walked to the back of the house.

"Shall we?" Z said, motioning to the drawing room. Rather than sit, I stood by the window and watched as the man out front spoke seemingly to no one. Must have a radio.

I turned to Z and George, who had both chosen to sit in chairs rather than side by side on the sofa. I felt like telling them they could; I wouldn't breathe a word about their previous—or current—dalliance. I didn't report on that sort of stuff. It was more my mother's former specialty.

"Ms. Cartwright, we understand that you had a connection to Mr. Sholes, the man found murdered in your flat," said George, her hands folded primly in her lap.

I rolled my eyes at the woman's demeanor. "For Christ's sake, let's just address the elephant in the room, as they say. I saw you and you saw me. While none of us knew one another then, we do now."

I could take or leave George, based on the woman's reaction, but Z intrigued me. The smug look on his face mirrored the way I was feeling at that moment.

"Let's cut to the chase," he said as he stood and walked closer to me. He stopped within a foot of where I was standing. "What did your father discover, and who would want him dead for it?"

For all my bravado of a minute ago, Z's direct question flummoxed me, even though I'd anticipated it. For some unknown reason, I couldn't bring myself to tell him I didn't know.

"We need to wait for Pinch," I said instead, catching the look that passed between Z and George. "I'm sure it won't be long before he returns."

"Excuse me," Z said when his mobile rang. He walked out of the room and exited through the front door. In less than two minutes, he was back.

"Change of plans," he barked. "We're leaving."

"What do you mean?" asked George.

"Heli will be here in five to transport us to Whittaker Abbey."

When George picked up her coat, Z looked at me. "You're going too."

"What about Pinch?"

"He's the one sending the heli."

I turned to go upstairs.

"Also, pack up whatever belongings you have here at Kingham. Pique will deliver them to the abbey. Be quick about it."

I wanted to tell Z where to stuff his demands, but held my tongue. I was partway up the stairs when I heard George speak to him in hushed tones.

"Has the location been compromised?"

"No."

"What's going on, then?"

"I wish I knew."

At least now I knew why Z hadn't extended the courtesy of explaining it to me—he didn't know himself.

It took the helicopter less than fifteen minutes to travel what would've taken almost two hours by car. When it landed, I saw Thornton Whittaker, Darrow's oldest brother and the current duke, waiting just outside the landing pad. The blades of the heli stopped spinning, and George escorted me over to him.

"Esland," he said. "It's nice to see you again. I'm sorry it's under these circumstances."

"Thank you, Your Grace."

He put his arm around my shoulders and gave me a pained smile. "Please call me something other than that."

"Yes, sir."

"How about Shiv?" he said, leading me toward the abbey.

I nodded.

"I'm going to apologize in advance on behalf of Losha and me, for our two children. Kazmir is a little boy who doesn't possess a filter of any kind, and Lilliya has no better volume control."

"I can't stay here," I blurted, wishing I'd had time to better phrase the words that flew from my brain and out of my mouth.

"I'm sorry. I'm making it sound so much worse than it is. Besides, Losha has set up the east wing for you, so if you'd rather not encounter our wee ones, you won't have to."

"I can't stay here," I repeated. "I know Pinch requested I be relocated, but it can't be here."

He put his hands on my shoulders and looked into my eyes. "For the time being, this is the safest place for you. I regret having to put it this way, but, Esland, you have no choice."

"I've already decided." I took a deep breath. "I'd prefer to return to town."

"There isn't a person here who would allow that to happen. You're in far too much danger."

"You would bring me into your home, where your wife and children are, knowing that? Are you daft?"

Shiver's expression eased from menacing. "I can assure you that I am not, although there are times my wife might disagree. You'll be staying with us, Esland, and I promise you, no harm will come to you or any of us as long as you're here. Come." He led me toward the abbey's entryway where a very beautiful woman waited.

"You must be Esland," she said. "I'm Orina, although my husband calls me Losha more often than not." The woman took my hand and then put her arm around my shoulders and led me inside. When Orina closed the door behind us, I stopped.

"As I told the duke, I cannot stay here, Your Grace."

The woman smiled. "As I'm sure Shiver told you, this is the safest place you can be, and please, call me Orina, or Losha. I answer to either."

The sitting room Orina led me into was one I recognized from when I used to visit Darrow here.

"Is she here?"

I heard a voice that sounded familiar, but I couldn't place it. Moments later, I was wrapped in the warm hug of Mrs. Mollybock, the Whittaker family's cook.

"Oh, my precious bairn," she said, brushing the hair from my face. "What can I bring you to eat? In case you still fancy it, I made that ghastly American dish you and Miss Darrow used to devour, especially at breakfast."

"You made mac and cheese?" I smiled.

"'Tisn't what the box says. There's no 'and,' missy. But yes, I did do."

"Thank you so much, Mrs. Mollybock, but I don't have much of an appetite."

"Come with me, lass, and I'll take care of that."

Orina motioned for me to go along.

Miss Molly, as Darrow and I used to call her, pulled out a chair in the kitchen, brought me a bowl of neon-orange-colored noodles—just like I remembered—and sat beside me. She jumped back up before I had time to pick up the fork she'd set next to the bowl, and came back with a glass of milk and a plate of what looked like warm cookies. Mrs. Mollybock then reached for the cup of tea she must've been drinking before she came out to the drawing room to collect me.

"How are you, Miss Esland?" she asked.

"Please, just call me Esland, or Ezzie, and honestly, I'm not well."

Ten minutes later, after I told her everything that had happened, Mrs. Mollybock picked up her third cookie, took a bite, and shook her head. "You are in quite a fix."

"I know."

The woman got up, filled the plate with more cookies, and brought it and a pitcher of milk to the table. It was just like I remembered when Darrow and I would beg to eat in the kitchen with Miss Molly rather than in the main dining room.

"Why is it you keep boxed macaroni and cheese?"

"Oh, lass. I keep it on hand in case Miss Darrow fancies some…what does she call it? Comfort food."

I smiled. "Just being here is comforting." But I couldn't stay, and I said as much.

"Now, now, lass. You must stay here."

"But they have children."

Mrs. Mollybock smiled. "That they do, but I understand the duchess asked for the east wing bedrooms to be prepared. You won't hear a peep from them."

"You misunderstand. I'm worried for their safety."

"I don't misunderstand a thing," she said, patting my hand. "Plus, Miss Darrow will get a kick out of the two of you having a slumber in her old rooms."

"Darrow? Is she here?"

"Not yet, lass, but I overheard the duke saying Mr. Axel would be delivering her this afternoon."

"I didn't know." My eyes inexplicably filled with tears.

"He cares so much for you, sweet bairn. He has since his dragon-slaying days."

"How did you know—"

"I've always known."

"That I had a crush on him?"

"Was more than that, and you know it."

"He didn't remember me."

"Maybe not your face, but it's your soul he recognized."

"That was so long ago."

"Yes, but he was your savior then, and again, he'll be."

I hardly remembered the days of which Mrs. Mollybock spoke. Darrow and I were likely no more than six or seven. Miss Molly was right; Axel, who was four years older, had slayed my dragons on a daily basis. Never Darrow's, though, who always insisted she could handle the task on her own.

"True!" shouted Darrow, running into the kitchen and hugging me. "It's so bloody good to see you," she added. "Although I hate the reason why with every fiber of my being."

"I'm so sorry," I said, taking a step back.

"That was always your way, wasn't it? Apologizing for things beyond your control." Darrow released me and hugged Mrs. Mollybock.

"Can I steal her?"

The cook smiled. "On your way, then."

Darrow took me by the hand and led me over to the east wing and up to the bedroom we used to stay in when I visited the abbey as a child.

She sat on the bed, pulled me next to her, and fell back on the mattress. "Remember all the nights we stayed awake until dawn, solving the world's problems? You were going to be the intrepid reporter—well done, by the way, crack reporter at the *Times* before the age of thirty. I always mean to tell you how proud I am of you."

"Thank you," I murmured.

"I was going to be the female equivalent of James Bond. I'm not there yet, but I'm working on it."

"What do you mean?"

"This has to stay so far off the record. You cannot utter it to any other living person."

"I would never, but if you can't tell me…"

"Of course I'll tell you. We're best mates."

I fell back on the mattress too, and stared at the ceiling. "You may not think so much longer."

"Oh, True, please do me the courtesy of begging that I tell you what I've been doing."

I gave Darrow a half-hearted smile. "Do tell."

Darrow rolled to her side like I had. "I've been at Fort Monckton."

"Fort Monckton?"

"As a reporter, you of all people should know that it's the SIS training site."

"In Portsmouth?"

Darrow rolled her eyes. "No, in Iceland," she responded sarcastically.

"Why?"

"Why am I training there, or why am I in training?"

"Both."

"I suppose it began with me being so bloody frustrated that I was left out of every single conversation that took place between my brothers and Axel. And then it got worse. Losha, Thornton's wife, was a Russian assassin, and as you know, Sutton's wife is a freaking genius NSA agent. Or was. Even my mother is living with Sir Ranald—what a scandal that was, right?"

I nodded. The truth was, I hadn't been paying much attention to the news of the duchess and Sir Ranald's affair; I'd assumed it for so long, although I couldn't say exactly why.

"Anyway, I'd had enough. Not just with that, but with everything. I escaped to America, came back due to Wellie's poor health, and in less than a month, my irrelevance was back in full force. And then, on New Year's Eve…"

"What happened?"

"You know Sutton and Wren were married that night?"

"I do."

"Everything was jolly, good fun until Axel and Quint ganged up on me. They were both wankered, and my so-called frivolous approach to life suddenly became their folly."

"Oh, dear."

"Right? Anyway, I was bloody angry and left. Eventually, Axel came looking for me, followed shortly thereafter by Quint. The two got into a pissing match and didn't even notice I'd left again."

"Then what happened?"

"I didn't sleep much at all. I went from feeling as though I finally mastered a certain independence—granted I was staying with Wren and Quint—but there I was, back in the same spot where I felt as though I'd lost myself. So, I disappeared."

"Wow." I shook my head. "Where did you go?"

"Nowhere. Wren and Wilder were off on their honeymoon. Quint was off my list anyway, so I ended up getting quite trolleyed at St. Ermin's. Evidently, after several days of unabashed eating and drinking, I called Axel, who came and got me." Darrow sighed. "Always the savior."

"How did you end up at Fort Monckton?"

"Once I sobered up, he listened to me, maybe for the first time. He actually paid attention and took me seriously, something I never expected him to do."

I felt as though a knife was piercing my heart, but at least now I knew that Axel and Darrow weren't as over as he'd said they were.

"He's the one who got me the training spot. Called in a favor from an old mate who, by the way, is now a bloody general. He gave me a couple of days on my own to think it over, and when I told him it was what I really wanted to do, he made it happen."

"Do you like it?"

"It is training, but yes, I love it."

"I'm sorry he interrupted it."

"You're more important, True." Darrow turned so she was facing me. "There are things you need to know about Axel and me."

"There are things I need to tell you about Axel and me too."

"You have always crushed on him," said Darrow, sitting up, perhaps to avoid looking me in the eye.

"We were children."

Darrow's shoulders rose and fell with a deep breath. "I know," she whispered. "I also knew he…it…was a bit more for him, no matter our age."

I shook my head.

"It was and I always knew it. It shames me to think that I let our friendship drift just to keep the two of you apart."

I had no idea how to respond. Would arguing that I believed Darrow wrong have any point? "He loves you," I said instead.

"Yes, he does, and I love him, but not in the way you mean."

"How, then?"

Darrow took another deep breath. "So many ways. We grew up together. I can't say he was like my brother, and I doubt he'd say it either. I know now how wrong I was to think we could ever have a romantic relationship, not in the long term anyway."

"What makes you say that?"

Darrow fell back against the mattress again and looked up at the ceiling. "There are innumerable reasons, but how could I have fallen for Quint so quickly if I was in love with Axel?"

"Are you with Quint now?"

Darrow shook her head. "I'm not with anyone now. I guess you could say that I'm with me. She doesn't know it, but Orina is the one who made me see it was something I had to do."

"How?"

"She told me that she and my brother would never have had a chance if they both hadn't first learned that they could exist on their own. Knew themselves better than they tried to know anyone else. She said she'd come to the realization that she didn't need Thornton, but she wanted him." Darrow rolled to her side. "I didn't know myself at all. I still don't, but I'm working on it."

I sighed like Darrow had. "I don't know myself either."

She smiled. "You've known yourself since you were a child. There are those of us who are babes of the universe, like me. I can be totally and utterly clueless. And then there are the old souls. You're one of them. You have wisdom that isn't of your years."

"You give me far too much credit. I am as clueless as any other."

"Axel is an old soul too. I think that's why you connected the way you did, even as children. So tell me, what happened between you?"

"We kissed—almost."

"Nothing more."

"No, nothing more."

"I wasn't asking, True. I know it was nothing more. You wouldn't allow it to be, because of me."

"Darrow, we aren't...I mean, he's helping me. That's all it is. In fact, doing so is his job."

She studied me and shook her head. "Oh, True, you are a silly thing at times. Listen to me very carefully."

"Okay."

"I'm not talking about the break-in or even the dead bloke found in your flat. I'm talking about you and Axel."

"If you have a single objection…"

Darrow shook her head. "How could I?"

"I'll gladly stay away from him if that's what you want."

"No, I don't want you to stay away from him, nor do I want him to stay away from you. There is no chance that Axel and I will ever have a romantic relationship again, and that's because *neither* of us wants it."

"That doesn't mean he wants one with me either."

Darrow laughed. "You were right a minute ago when you said you were as clueless as any other, but only in this. Open your eyes, my dear friend, and take a look at the man when he's in front of you. He has the same dazed, love-filled expression you do when you talk about him."

"He doesn't love me, nor I, him. That's ludicrous."

"Maybe not yet, but ultimately, it's what you both want. Especially Axel."

"How do you know this?"

"Because we spent the entire ride from Portsmouth here talking about you."

13

Pinch

When I heard Darrow and Esland run up the stairs, I went into the sitting room where Z and George were waiting.

"What in bloody hell is going on?" Z asked, standing when I entered the room.

"Sit back down and I'll explain." I turned to George, who also stood. "You too."

In a matter of minutes, I'd briefed them both on what I believed Esland knew, which was very little. "From what I understand, Sholes came to her about her parents' death, telling her it wasn't an accident."

"Why now?" George asked.

"My understanding is he was very ill."

"He told her nothing else?" asked Z.

"Only that when he knew more, she would too. There was someone he believed could help them, but he didn't tell her who."

"Help them do what?"

"Finish what her father started, I suppose."

"What's your plan?" Z asked, his tone less accusatory than it had been.

"Help her figure out what it was."

"What about—"

Before George could say anything more, Z held up his hand. "Who do you want on the team?"

"Pique and Edge for now. My plan is to take her out of the country once I've returned Darrow to Monckton. If you can spare Grinder and Rile, it would be helpful."

Z smiled. "I had a feeling that's where she'd gone."

"Sure you did." I laughed. "You also knew that wasn't where she went first."

He laughed as well. "You got me there, Pinch."

George stood, clearing her throat. "This is all well and good, but I've got—"

"We'll discuss it on our way back to London," said Z, interrupting her a second time.

I had no idea what was up between them and really couldn't have cared less. As long as Z was willing to let me pursue the investigation into Esland's parents' death, and give me the support I needed to do so, George could bloody well sod off as far as I was concerned.

"If that's all, I think I'll pay my father a visit."

Z walked over and put his hand on my shoulder. "Please give Wellie my regards, and, Pinch, whatever you need, don't hesitate to let me know."

I caught the third look of utter dismay on George's face. Perhaps she'd done something to piss Z off. There was little other explanation I could come up with as to why Z was being so short with the woman who was my rival for the man's former job.

"We'll take the heli back to London," Z said, walking out with me. "Oh, and tell your father I'm almost out of brandy."

"Hello, Pops," I said, walking in the front door of his cottage.

"Well, if it isn't my boy." My father rose from the chair he always sat in and walked over to where I stood. "How are you, son?" he asked, embracing me.

So often, I wished I could be as free with my affection as my father was. He'd never once hesitated to hug me or say that he loved me.

"I'm not great, to be honest."

My father walked into the kitchen, pulled his signature unmarked bottle from the shelf, and poured us both a glass.

"I'm not sure a shot of brandy is always the answer, Pops."

"It never is. It just makes finding them easier."

I smiled and drank the shot he poured.

"Come, sit, and tell me what's on your mind."

My father slowly made his way to his chair. It troubled me to see the evident pain he was in. "How are you feeling?"

"Good days and bad."

"Are you eating properly?"

"Mrs. Mollybock makes sure I have what I need." My father grinned and patted his belly. "And then some. That reminds me, fancy some stew?"

"I'm not hungry, Pops, but eat if you are."

"Tell me what's on your mind first."

"Darrow and I are finished."

My father brushed his finger over his lips. "That is not what's troubling you."

I smiled. "You're right. It isn't." I got up and walked over to the shelf where the framed photo of me with Grant Cartwright sat and picked it up.

I remembered that day so vividly now that I'd had the reminder of it.

Darrow had talked Esland into asking her father for tickets to a sold-out match. Duchess Whittaker, Darrow's mum, had pitched quite a fit about her daughter's audacity, but in the end, Esland secured the tickets.

I didn't remember seeing much of the two girls once we arrived at the stadium; I'd been too excited about seeing my first match in person. Now that I thought about it, I remembered Esland bringing her father to the side of the field where we sat and security escorting us through the gate for the photo.

How had I forgotten her entirely?

"Shame about the accident," I heard my father say. "He was in the prime of his life and career. And poor True, losing both her parents."

"You remember what Darrow used to call her? I didn't."

My father continued brushing his lips with his fingertips, waiting for me to go on.

"She came to me to ask for help, and I turned her away."

"With what?"

"She has reason to believe the accident that took her parents' lives wasn't one at all."

"There was speculation at the time, but the coroner determined it had been."

"Evidently, there's new reason to think otherwise."

"Are you saying they were murdered?"

"It seems he had something on the football league that it is believed got him killed."

"Is True in danger herself?"

"She is, Pops. A great deal of it."

"Is MI5 investigating?"

"Yes."

"What is your role, son?"

"I don't have time for this, but I find I have no choice."

My father nodded. "You are handling this personally."

"Am I daft to?"

"Not at all. In fact, you are doing exactly as you should."

"There are others very well qualified who could manage the investigation as well as her protection."

"None better than you."

"I appreciate the faith you have in me, Pops, but you know as well as I that I should oversee this case rather than be as hands-on as I am."

My father put his hands on either side of his chair. "Don't get up. Whatever you need, I'll get it."

"'Tis you that needs another shot, Axel. Not I."

"Because you believe me unreasonable?"

He smiled and shook his head. "Because I believe you too stubborn to recognize what's right in front of you."

"And that is?"

"You and True have had a connection since you were wee ones playing on the grounds of the estate. I remember the duke predicting that one day you'd lose your heart to her forever."

"That's a bloody fabrication." I smiled and so did he.

"I swear on your mother's soul," he said, crossing himself.

I never understood why he did that. My father wasn't a religious man as far as I knew.

"Open your eyes to what's right in front of you, son. It's already been lost."

"I kissed her—well, I tried to anyway."

He nodded as though this came as no surprise to him. "I love you, Axel."

"I love you too, Pops."

14

Esland

"Trust Axel, and do whatever he tells you to do," said Darrow.

"Listen to her."

I looked toward the bedroom door and saw him leaning against the jamb. Instead of looking at him too, Darrow studied me.

"What?"

"You've done the right thing, True. You just need to see it through."

"I'd forgotten that's what you used to call her," said Axel, walking over to the bedroom window. "Why did you?"

"My name means true," I responded.

Darrow jumped up. "I haven't seen Wellie, yet. I think I'll go do that. I mean, unless there's something else you need me for, or if I'm not allowed to."

"What are you going on about?" Pinch asked her.

"When are we going to Monckton?"

"Not until tomorrow."

Darrow clapped her hands, leaned down, and kissed my cheek.

I watched Axel as my friend scurried off, looking for any sign of a lingering connection between them. I could honestly say that if I met them together on the street, my first impression would be that they were siblings.

"Hi," he said, slowly stalking toward me. It was only a few steps, yet it seemed an endless time before he was close enough to touch.

"Hi," I answered, standing to meet him. "You went to get her."

"I did."

"Just to prove to me that the two of you are no longer a couple?"

"I hope I was successful."

"It was a little extreme, don't you think? I mean, you could've just let me call her."

He smiled. "I wanted her to tell you in person."

I sat in the chair by the window and covered my face with my hands.

"Tell me what you're thinking," he said, sitting on the ledge that formed a window seat.

"What about when this is over?"

"When what's over?"

"When you no longer have to protect me. When we both go back to our lives, the ones in which I annoy the bloody hell out of you."

"I can't answer that," he said, leaning forward and resting his elbows on his knees. "I know what I want to happen."

I cringed and closed my eyes. "What is that?"

He put his hand on my arm. "Look at me, Ezzie."

I opened my eyes, not expecting him to be so close.

"I want to get to know you better; I'd like you to get to know me better."

"And in the meantime?"

"We unravel the mystery of who killed Tommy Sholes and your parents."

I nodded. I was actually going to do this, and not alone—Axel would be with me.

"And I keep you safe."

I felt the warmth of his touch spread throughout my body when he grasped my neck.

"I feel as though I've waited forever to do this. I'm going to kiss you now, Ezzie."

I didn't wait for him. Instead, I brought my lips to his.

He pulled me out of the chair and up against him. One hand cupped my cheek, and the other rested on my bottom. He crushed his mouth to mine, and I groaned. His hand moved to tangle in my hair, tugging my head back. His day's worth of stubble left a smoldering burn on my neck when his teeth scraped along my throat.

He took my hand and led me away from the window. When his gaze raked over me, lavishing his steamy attention on me, my nipples strained against my bra and my knickers moistened.

"You're coming with me when I take Darrow to Monckton."

"Okay."

"We won't be coming back here, at least not right away."

"When will we leave?"

He brought his mouth to mine again, forcing his tongue between my lips. When he pulled away, I forgot I'd asked a question.

"One hour."

Rather than being disappointed, Darrow seemed giddy about going to Fort Monckton even though Axel had said earlier that we wouldn't leave until tomorrow.

After saying her goodbyes, she opened the back passenger door of the 4x4 sitting near the abbey's entryway.

"I can sit in the back," I offered.

At the same time Darrow shook her head and climbed inside, Axel pushed me up against the outside of the vehicle.

"You'll sit in front with me." He crushed his mouth to mine like he had earlier. When he stepped away, I thought about asking if that was for Darrow's benefit, but I stopped myself. There'd be more than enough time for that conversation once we dropped her off at training and were alone.

"In, you go," he said, opening my door.

"You two are explosive, True," said Darrow from behind me as Axel walked around to get in on the driver's side.

"I'm sorry. That was insensitive."

"Hot is what it was."

"What?" asked Axel when he fastened his lap belt.

I smirked. As if he didn't know.

Periodically on our two-hour drive, Axel would reach over and rest his hand on my thigh. Each time he did, our eyes met in a lustful gaze. If Darrow noticed, she didn't comment.

"Remember when we used to pick barrelsful of apples and then hurl them at Sutton and Axel?" Darrow asked.

"The rottener, the better as I recall," Axel commented. "As you two were."

When I stuck my tongue out at him, the look on his face went from playful to heated, and he moved his hand farther up my thigh.

Even back then, I'd crushed on him. When Darrow told me that she and Axel were secretly dating, I'd been crushed instead. I looked away from him with the memory.

I felt his fingers squeeze my thigh, but didn't turn toward him. While Darrow may say she was okay with our burgeoning relationship, that didn't mean I could simply forget that before his hands were on my body, they had been on Darrow's. I shook my head against the mental image, but it remained.

15

Pinch

I willed the kilometers to pass more quickly, so I could address whatever was going on with Esland. She'd gone from flirty to sullen in a matter of seconds.

My eyes met Darrow's when I looked in the mirror, and she shrugged.

Since going back and changing the past wasn't an option, I'd spend the next few days convincing Esland that everything about her consumed me. My thoughts revolved solely around her and her safety.

I took in the countryside as I drove, wondering how it could be so easy to go from loving one person to complete infatuation with another.

Perhaps if I'd been with Esland first, and she broke things off with me, it wouldn't have been easy at all.

"Wellie told me that he and my father once predicted that you two would end up together," Darrow said from the back seat. The comment got Esland to turn her head, first toward me and then toward Darrow.

"He told me the same thing," I said.

"How odd," murmured Esland.

"I don't think it's odd," said Darrow. "I think it's obvious."

I met her gaze in the mirror a second time and subtly shook my head. She couldn't see Esland's face and, thus, didn't realize she was doing more damage than good.

We rode in relative silence the rest of the way.

"You take good care of True," Darrow said when I parked near Monckton's main building and she hugged me.

Esland had gotten out of the 4x4 too, and the two women embraced. Something passed between them, but I couldn't hear their words.

Soon we were back on the road, and Esland was as quiet as she'd been before.

"We'll travel another two hours and then stop for the night. It'll allow for a shorter time on the road tomorrow."

"Okay," she mumbled.

I took her hand in mine. "Talk to me, Ezzie. Tell me what's on that stunning mind of yours."

She took a deep breath. "Nothing."

"Try again."

"You're right. There is a lot on my mind. I guess that's not surprising, given there's a person, or persons, out there who wants to kill me."

"I'll repeat; try again, Esland. Tell me what's bothering you about us."

It took her a long time to answer, but since we'd be on the road for another two hours, I could wait.

"The simplest way I can put this is, how would you feel if I'd had a dalliance with Sutton."

Dalliance. I smiled. "He'd be long since dead."

"I'm serious, Pinch."

"Axel."

"For Christ's sake, you don't have to do that every time. I know your name. What difference does it make?"

She was angry with me, but now I was angry with her too.

"It makes a difference to me. This isn't work, Esland. This is personal. My name is Axel. When I'm at MI5, I'm Pinch."

"Okay, *Axel,* how would you feel if I'd had a relationship with Sutton?"

"I'd hate it. I would've hated it from the moment it started."

"Then, you know how I feel."

"Did you really hate it?"

"More than it's possible to say."

"I'm sorry." I brought her hand to my lips. "Tell me, Ezzie, how can we get past this?"

"It's awkward, that's all."

I smiled and turned her hand over to kiss her palm. "I'm glad to hear that's all it is."

"I gave her the chance to have you back, and she turned it down."

I could swear my heart warmed with her words, and her smile made it hotter. Perhaps I should stop sooner and not try to get all the way to Maidstone tonight.

"Where are we going?" Esland asked when I turned off the motorway a few minutes later.

"There's an inn where Winston Churchill used to stay not far from here."

"Westbrook?"

"You know it?"

"My parents used to take me there on holiday. Are you aware of the Ian Fleming room?" she asked, leaning her head against the back of the seat.

She was smiling; Westbrook brought back good memories for her. "Is that where you stayed?"

"My father always booked the Garden House for us."

"I understand it's quite lovely."

"You've been to Westbrook though, haven't you?"

"Never."

That seemed to please her. Maybe because she didn't have to speculate if I'd been there with Darrow.

"I'm quite weary of driving. I thought it might be a nice place to stop for the night." I doubted it would be busy at this time of year, but one never knew with swanky places such as this.

I pulled up to the portico, came around, opened Esland's door, and held out my hand.

"Thank you."

I kissed the back of it when she placed it in mine, and then turned it over to kiss her palm like I had before.

Esland didn't try to pull away. Her gaze rested on the place where my lips met her skin.

Once inside, I checked with the desk while Esland sought out the lavatory.

"Is there any availability in the Garden House?" I asked the clerk.

"Whichever room you'd like, sir," the man answered.

"Meaning none of the rooms are booked?"

"That's correct. Would you like to stay in the main house?"

"We'll take the Garden House."

"All of it, sir?"

"That's right."

The clerk clicked away on the computer keyboard while I fidgeted, hoping Esland wouldn't return until I was finished, so I could surprise her.

"How many nights?"

"When is your next reservation?"

"Let's see." The man studied the screen for some time. "Nothing for two weeks out, sir."

I set my credit card on the keyboard. "We'll stay a week for the time being. We may decide to stay on longer."

The man cleared his throat at the same time I heard Esland's footfalls.

"That will be more than—"

"That's fine."

"Do they have any rooms?" she asked, coming to stand behind me. When the clerk looked up, I shook my head just slightly.

"The dining room will be serving dinner for another hour if you'd like to partake while we prepare your accommodations," he suggested.

"I'm famished. What about you?" I asked.

Not only did Esland nod, she looked happier than I remembered ever seeing her before. It was as though the strain of what she'd been going through for the last several hours had been magically lifted away. If I could give her that gift for even a few days, I'd be a happy man.

"The menu hasn't changed," she announced once we were seated near a window in the dining room we appeared to have to ourselves.

"Is that a good thing?" I asked, not having looked at mine. I was too busy taking in how transformed Esland seemed by this place and the memories it evoked.

"It's a very good thing. I can't decide what to order since it's all so fabulous."

I thought about telling her she could work her way through her favorites since we'd be here at least a week, but decided to hold off on the surprise and deliver it with maximum impact.

The desk clerk came to our table as we were finishing dinner. "Your accommodations are ready, sir," he said, handing me a key.

Esland's eyes met mine. "Are we staying in the Garden House?"

"We are."

Her eyes filled with tears. "Thank you, Axel."

"Mmm."

"What?"

I took her hand in mine, brought it to my lips. "I like making you happy."

"Thank you," she said again, her cheeks flushing.

"Ready?"

The 4x4 was still parked under the portico. "Do you know how to get to the Garden House from here?"

She smiled. "In my sleep."

It was very dark, yet Esland navigated us straight to our accommodations. I pulled up in front and walked to the entrance.

"I should've asked…"

"What?"

"Are we…sharing a room?"

I cupped her cheek. "I would like nothing more, but—"

"It's okay," she said quickly. "I just wanted to be sure you hired two."

"We have the entire cottage."

There was a smile on her face, but it didn't shine through her eyes. She walked down the hallway, stopping at the first room she came to. "I'll sleep in here," she said without looking at me.

"Ezzie—"

"Don't," she said, her eyes filling with tears.

"I want you to understand—" Before I could utter another word, she closed the bedroom door in my face.

What was wrong with me? Why had I made her think I didn't want her when I'd never experienced such desire?

Because she mattered, I almost said aloud. Forty-eight hours ago, I'd dumped her on the sidewalk after threatening to kill her. Not that I'd meant it, but my anger was what had scared her.

Now, here she was, on the other side of the door I still stood outside of. I could be in there, next to her, finally feeling her naked body, if I hadn't hesitated, hadn't let her know without words that I thought it was too soon for us to sleep together.

I went out to the 4x4 and brought her trunk and my satchel inside. I walked to the bedroom door and rapped softly. "I have your things," I said when there was no response.

"Thank you," her soft voice answered.

I opened the door and stepped in the room. She put her head in her hands but not quickly enough for me to miss she'd been crying. My heart wrenched. I walked over and sat beside her, pulling her into my arms.

"I'm sorry."

"Oh, God," she cried, moving away from me. "Now you're pitying me?"

"No! That isn't it at all." I rubbed my hair with my hand before grasping her wrists with both hands. "You've been through so much. I can't—I won't—take advantage of your vulnerability more than I already have."

"You don't need to make excuses." She shook her head. "I knew I was right all along."

"What is that supposed to mean?"

"Now that you've seen Darrow, you realized she's who you really want."

"You've got to be kidding." I stood when she did, stalking over to stand in front of her. I pushed her up against the wall. "Does this ring any bells?" I asked before crushing my mouth against hers. I forced my tongue between her lips and angled my head to deepen our kiss.

When she turned her head away and wiped her mouth with the back of her hand, I dropped mine and backed away. I turned around and walked to the door.

"I want you to know I've never wanted to be with another woman more than I want to be with you," I said before crossing the threshold and closing the door behind me.

I went into the room next door after shutting off all but one light in the cottage. If Esland woke in the middle of the night and needed to find her way to the loo, I didn't want her fumbling around in the dark.

I took off my clothes, cursing my stupidity for the umpteenth time, and crawled into bed.

I woke with a start, having no idea what time it was or how long I'd been asleep. I tore out of the bed and ran into the room next door where Esland thrashed under her covers, uttering words I couldn't understand.

"Ezzie, wake up," I said, clutching both her wrists in one hand while the other stroked her cheek. "You're having a bad dream," I said when she opened her eyes and looked at me questioningly.

She tried to pull away, but I held her wrists, now with both hands.

"I'm sorry if I woke you," she muttered.

"You didn't," I lied, stretching out behind her in the slim space she'd left when she rolled over.

"What are you doing?" she said over her shoulder.

"If you have another nightmare, I want to be here to ease you out of it."

"You don't have to do this." She tried to scoot away, but all it did was give me more room to snuggle against her.

"I want to." I moved her hair out of my way and kissed the back of her neck. "Go to sleep, sweetness."

Esland was still asleep hours later when I eased out of bed to answer the phone I heard vibrating in the room I'd left it in.

"Pinch," I said, grabbing it before it woke her.

"Pique here."

"Do you have an update?"

"Not much yet. I wanted you to know I'm on premise with Edge and Rile. Other than by us, you weren't followed."

"Good."

"When will you be leaving?"

"I'm not certain yet, but it won't be today. Maybe not until the end of the week."

"Understood."

"In the meantime, have Grinder take a look at Willingham Allied, the whole league in fact, and see if you can dig anything up from eleven years ago. What scandals were there? Who was in trouble, both personally and with their respective team?"

"I can do it from here. Anything else?"

I rubbed my eyes with one hand. I'd been so soundly asleep, I felt groggy. "I'll get back to you on that."

"Understood."

I ended the call and crept back to the room where I hoped Esland still lay sleeping. I wanted nothing more than to crawl in beside her and feel her soft body next to mine.

Instead, I groaned when I saw the bed empty.

"Good morning," I said when I found her in the kitchen, rummaging through the cupboards and drawers.

"Good morning," she said, not looking at me.

"Ezzie?"

"Yes?"

I waited silently until she finally met my gaze. "What are you doing?"

"Trying to patch together something to eat before we have to leave."

She turned her head away, but I saw her tears. I walked over and took the bowl she was holding from her hands and set it on the table.

I leaned forward and touched her lips with mine. "We aren't leaving today."

"Didn't you say we had another day of driving?"

"Changed my mind. Plus, I like the smile this place brings to your beautiful face."

I loved that she went from frowning to smiling with the news.

Esland walked over to the kitchen door and opened it. "I should've known," she exclaimed, reaching down to pick up a basket that sat inside the porch.

"What's that?"

"Breakfast!" She moved the cloth aside and pulled out scones, lemon curd, and fruit. "They're still warm," she moaned, bringing a piece of scone to her lips.

When I stepped closer, she broke another piece off and offered it to me. I took it in my mouth, nipping at her fingers as I did.

She giggled again and turned to fill the tea kettle with water. "Fancy a cup?" she asked.

"Please." I sat at the table, watching as she moved around the kitchen as if she lived here. "Tell me about a typical day here with your parents."

"After breakfast, we'd play tennis. My mother was much better at it than my father, so he and I were a team against her. She always won, of course, but that really wasn't the point of it. My father would be so silly, he'd bring her to tears of laughter."

"Then what?"

"We'd go exploring. There are secret gardens everywhere, like those at Whittaker Abbey. Once, we even found a tree house. I wonder if I could find it again."

"I say we should try."

"I'd like that." She smiled, leaned forward, and kissed my cheek. "Thank you for bringing me here, Axel."

It was the happiest of accidents, but as my father would say, they rarely were. He believed that the hand of God and his angels directed people where they should go. He also believed that those same angels brought the people together who should be.

"You're welcome," I said, longing to give her a real kiss. "Tell me more."

"If the weather was bad, my mother would write and my father would take me to the main house to watch movies. I wonder if the cinema is still operational."

I walked out to the entryway, grabbed the card I'd noticed the night before, and brought it into the kitchen. "It is."

"Really? What's playing?"

I laughed. "This afternoon there's a run of *Four Weddings and a Funeral,* and this evening's feature is Dr. No."

I handed her the card so she could see the rest of the week's schedule.

"Oh."

"What?"

"It's nothing," she said, setting the card on the table behind her.

"Tell me."

"*The Third Man* is playing later in the week. So like I said, nothing."

"A personal favorite?"

She shook her head, but I knew it was. I looked forward to watching it with her in order to figure out what about it intrigued her.

"I think I saw Monty Python on the bill for tomorrow evening."

"I didn't notice," she said, turning back to finish putting our breakfast on the table. "Will we leave tomorrow?"

"I hope not."

She cocked her head.

"I'd like to stay on a couple more days at least."

"Really?" Her smile broadened.

"You love it here."

Her cheeks flushed. "I do. I doubted I'd ever be back."

"And here you are."

Her stomach growled and she giggled. It was a lovely sound.

16

Esland

It was midwinter, but the grounds of Westbrook were still breathtaking. Every step I took brought back a memory of something I'd forgotten.

There was a large pond stocked with trout where my father and I had fished and I'd caught my first. There was a field where I'd learned to shoot clay pigeons. The gardens and woodlands had matured since I last visited, but the basic structure of the estate remained unchanged enough that I knew my way around.

We hadn't found the tree house yet, but Axel was diligent about looking in every tree we passed.

"There it is," he shouted a few minutes later, pointing.

I came back to where he stood and looked up.

"What's wrong?"

"That isn't it."

"Tree." He touched the bark and then pointed. "House."

"Yes, but not the one I remember."

"Is there more than one?"

"I think, yes. Maybe."

"Cor blimey," he muttered and kept walking.

"You say that a lot."

"Favorite expression of Wellie's."

"Is that what you call him?"

"Wellie? No."

"What, then?"

"Pops."

"You're kidding."

He shook his head. "No. Why?"

"It's what I called my father."

He smiled and continued looking up into every tree we passed.

"We don't have to find it today. We don't have to find it at all," I told him, a handful of paces later.

"It's become imperative."

I laughed. "Why?"

"I don't know."

"Now I know why they call you Pinch."

He stopped walking and grabbed my hand, pulling me around to look at him.

"Why?"

I put my hands on either side of his mouth and squeezed. "Because when you're focused on something, your face pinches."

Axel smiled and leaned forward to kiss me. "That isn't why, but we'll have to wait until later for me to show you the real reason."

My eyes bored into his. If I told him that's what I wanted, would he pull away from me again? I couldn't take another round of rejection. I tried, but he wrapped his arm around my waist and pulled me back into him.

"Ezzie?"

He cupped my face and kissed me again. I didn't pull away this time when his tongue pushed its way into my mouth. Instead, I pushed back and kissed him harder.

"God, woman. Do you have any idea how much I like kissing you?"

"I like kissing you too."

When I shivered, he tightened his grasp.

"Cold?" he asked.

"Not really," I said, looking down at the ground.

"What, then?" he asked, lifting my chin to look at him.

"I'd like to know why they call you Pinch."

17

Pinch

There was hesitation evident in her voice. "But?"

"There's something I need you to know."

I moved my hands to her hips, digging my fingers into her flesh. It was all I could do not to toss her over my shoulder like I had at the pub, and carry her to the cottage.

"Axel."

My lips drifted to her neck; I licked her skin and nipped my way from her neck to her shoulder.

"Please," she said, wriggling away from me and standing with her hands on the same hips I'd just held. "I need you to listen to me."

"I'm listening," I said while at the same time trying to rein in my desire to take her right there in the forest.

"This might mean more to me than it does to you."

"I can assure you, that isn't the case."

"Before things…go any further…I need you to know…I care about you, Axel."

"I care about you too, Ezzie."

"If we do this, you have to understand that it won't be just sex for me."

"It wouldn't be for me either." I felt like all I was doing was repeating her words back to her, but I meant them as much as she did. Esland took a breath like she was going to say more, but I put my finger on her lips before she could.

"I need you to listen to me for a minute."

She nodded, but I didn't move my finger.

"I could've handed your detail over to any one of the guys who was at Kingham with us, but I didn't. What's more, I couldn't. When I drove to Monckton to pick up Darrow, I hated being away from you. The entire way back, I couldn't wait to see you. That's why I called for the heli to take you, Z, and George to the abbey. I simply couldn't wait. And when Darrow sprinted up to see you first, I was envious that she would get to spend time with you before I did." I moved my fingers from her lips. "It was worse than that. I know this is the last thing I should say to you right now, but it was never like this with her. Never. Not even in the beginning."

Esland's eyes were focused on mine.

"Please say something," I begged.

"I'm trying to figure out the right way to say it without making you feel bad."

"Bugger me," I muttered.

"First, that was exactly what I needed to hear. And exactly what I didn't."

"I'm sorry—"

"Wait," she said, putting her fingers on my lips. It was all I could do not to run my tongue over the tips.

"I can't hear about you and Darrow. Maybe never again."

I nodded.

"But knowing it's different between us, that was the part I needed to hear." She moved her fingers away. "You can talk now."

"I don't want to talk," I growled.

"What do you want to do?"

"This." I had my hands on her before she could say another word. I lifted her so her legs went around my waist. "I need you, Ezzie. I want you so much, I'm ready to rip these clothes from your body."

"Do it."

I let her slide down the front of me. Instead of tearing the clothes she wore, I led her to the cottage.

Once there, I pushed her up against the wall of the entryway, grinding my body into hers. "I need to know you're sure about this, Ezzie."

Rather than answer, she kissed me hard and brought my hand to her breast. "Please, Axel."

I picked her up and carried her into the first bedroom I came to, set her on her feet, and walked her backwards until she fell against the bed. Only then did I remove her clothes, slowly, piece by piece.

Her body was strong and lean, like an athlete's. My guess was it came to her naturally, like it had to her father. No matter where I touched her, the skin was soft, but underneath, the muscles were corded.

I rested my still-clothed body between her legs and worked my way down from her neck with my lips.

Her breasts were the perfect size. Plump and full— the way I liked them to be. I laved her left nipple while my fingers plucked the right, and her body began to move against me.

"You like this," I murmured, changing sides. "So do I. I could do this for hours."

"Please," she begged, arching her body so my hardness rested against her sex.

"Patience, Ezzie," I told her, continuing my way down her abs to her belly button.

"God, Axel, I feel like I've wanted you forever," she breathed. "Please don't make me wait any longer."

"Since you asked so nicely…" I smiled and stood to remove my clothes. I pulled a condom from my pocket, ripped the foil with my teeth, and rolled it on my cock while she watched. Her eyes were hooded, but they stayed focused on everything I did, everywhere I touched.

When I positioned myself at her entrance, I could feel how ready she was for me. I slowly eased in, watching a flush spread up her skin. Nothing—no one—had ever felt like this. Her body was made for mine. A perfect fit.

"Still," I whispered when she tried to angle herself to feel me deeper. There was no way I'd hurry. Now that I was finally exactly where I was supposed to be, with the woman whose body, mind, heart, and soul I now knew belonged to me, I wanted to linger, feeling everything, so I'd remember how this felt for the rest of my life.

When I looked into her eyes, I swore I saw the same emotion, the same acknowledgment that now our bodies were joined together, there would never be anyone else for either of us.

18

Esland

Could he really be thinking the same thing I was? The way he looked at me said he did.

I'd fantasized about him so many times. About being with him like this, and yet, it was so much better than any dream, any expectation I may have had.

I wanted him to go harder, faster, deeper, while at the same time, soft, slow, languid, like he was now. I wanted to feel everything from Axel. Make love every way he liked, do everything he wanted, share all of myself with him.

He stopped and kissed my lips, my cheeks, the tip of my nose, and each of my eyelids. "Look at me, Ezzie," he said. "Look into my eyes and tell me what you see."

I couldn't respond because what I saw was love—deep, pure, committed love. Was I wrong? I had to be; less than a week ago, he detested me. How could he love me now?

He moved again, agonizingly slow, peering into my eyes, waiting for me to answer.

"Tell me, Esland. What do you see?"

"You care about me."

He stopped again, smiling. "Is that all?"

"Please, Axel. Don't."

He moved again, but didn't pick up his pace. "Okay, I'll tell you what I see."

He kissed me again, this time tangling his tongue with mine and thrusting deeper inside me.

"Tell me, Axel."

"So many things, my beautiful girl. I see trust and I see acceptance. But most importantly, I see love. How long has it been, Ezzie, since we fell in love? Was it when we were children? Did we know, like my father did, that one day the universe would bring us together like it did now?"

"I did, until—"

He covered my mouth with his to silence me. "Tell me when you fell in, not when you fell out."

"As long as I can remember."

"Me too."

He began to move in earnest, building in strength and depth. "Let me see you, Ezzie. Show me your pleasure."

The sun was coming up when he finally let me sleep. Every inch of me felt as sated as sore. We'd never said the words; it was too soon. It was one thing to say we loved each other, but to bring it to being in love was a step I wasn't ready to take, at least in words.

19

Pinch

Ezzie stretched her arms above her head. "I need sustenance."

"Think there'll be another basket left on the kitchen porch?"

"Definitely."

She climbed out of bed, and instead of grabbing clothes, she sauntered out of the room without a stitch on, heading toward the kitchen rather than the lavatory. Intrigued, I followed; however, I donned my trousers before doing so.

I stood in the doorway, leaning up against the jamb as I watched her navigate the kitchen, marveling at how comfortable she was in her own skin. More so than me, and wasn't it the gent who was supposed to prefer wandering the house naked?

The kettle whistled, and a minute later, she set a cup and saucer on the table.

"This is yours," she said.

I walked over and took a seat. Before she could walk away, I grabbed her arm and pulled her onto my lap.

"I like seeing you like this."

"Domesticated?" She laughed.

"Naked."

"Oh." Her cheeks flushed. Now she was embarrassed? "I'm not big on clothes. I suppose I should've warned you."

"Not big on clothes." I shook my head, smiling. "Define that for me."

"It isn't like I'd run outside this way. I'm not a nudist, but if I'm home, I'm far more comfortable in as few clothes as possible."

I brought my fingers to her right nipple and brushed her neck with the scruff of my beard. "You are so bloody sexy," I growled. "I'm tempted to spend the next several days inside this cottage and never step out. However, I'm anxious to find this tree house of yours."

Esland pulled back and looked in my eyes. "Several?"

"Will you grow bored?"

"Never. I could live here, given the choice." Her eyes filled with tears. When one ran down her cheek, I brushed it away with the pad of my thumb.

"Tell me why you're crying."

"You're being so nice to me."

The words were screaming inside my head, but something kept me from saying them. My heart was full of love. Whether she was ready to hear that, I doubted, but there was no purer truth. "I'm sorry I wasn't always," I said instead.

"You really didn't make the connection between the Esland of our childhood and the reporter?"

"I didn't. Darrow always called you True. It never occurred to me that it wasn't your name."

"It wasn't like we ever had a formal introduction."

"I am sorry I didn't realize sooner."

"Maybe it was meant to go this way."

"How so?"

"If we'd ever gone out on a double, I doubt I'd be sitting naked on your lap now."

"Ah." The idea of her with another man made my shoulders tight. I was beginning to see why she didn't want to hear about my time with Darrow. The truth was, she'd handled it so much better than I would've.

"What are you thinking?" she asked, studying me.

"I would've put you over my shoulder, just like I did at the pub, and carried you away. Only I wouldn't have left you there; I would've taken you home with me."

She laughed. "And what of Darrow?"

"She'd have right killed me." I brought my lips to hers. "Would've been worth it though, just to get a taste of you."

Esland angled her head and kissed me harder than I had her. "Take me back to bed, Axel," she pleaded.

"How could I ever say no to you?"

"Still all clear," Pique said when he answered my call a few hours later. I'd sneaked away when Ezzie fell asleep.

"Good. I'd like to stay here for a few more days if we can. What about her flat?"

"It's being watched, but my guess is they've hired a PI to do it. Same with the *Times*."

As long as no one knew Esland was here in Surrey, I'd take advantage of the time I was able to spend alone with her.

"What have you found on Willingham Allied or any of their players specifically?"

"The same thing that plagues most competitive sports—bribery, fixed games, dirty players, doping."

With billions of pounds on the line, there were innumerable allegations of everything Pique mentioned.

"Any in trouble on WA now?"

"Bale Zeko is always in the headlines, but so far, none of the allegations against him have stuck."

Zeko was considered the number one player in the world, so as Pique said, it wasn't a surprise that he'd be accused. No one would make better headlines than he.

"Wasn't there something in the news about an underage prostitute?"

"Trumped up by Liverpool."

"Remind me what happened again."

"Zeko and four other players were accused of having sex with an underage girl. All five swore they hadn't, but she told a pretty convincing tale. I think it was the *Times* that uncovered the conspiracy and proved the men innocent."

"Was it Esland's byline?"

"I'd have to check, but I don't believe so."

"What about doping? Anything on that?"

"The WADA does random checks on players throughout the league. When it comes to the World Cup, the testing intensifies."

"Zeko ever come up dirty?"

"Negative."

"Anyone who did?"

"Stone Olivier from Lorrington City was dinged, but that was for cocaine."

"Right." I remembered the headlines. Cocaine use had plagued the league for years, back to before Esland's father's accident. It didn't carry the same stigma as performance-enhancing doping though. Most often the players who used the drug were seen as *gobshites* more than cheaters.

"What about back in Graham's day?" I asked.

"Same *shite*, different decade, Pinch. He was never accused, though."

"What about Tommy Sholes?"

"Negative."

Graham Cartwright had never been "just a footballer." He had been a national hero. And while national heroes fell from grace every day, something told me that Esland's father never would have.

But if Pique and I were on the right track, would any of the run-of-the-mill allegations result in murder? Probably not, unless there was proof, and even then, it couldn't be accusations against one person. It had to be wider spread.

"As far as anything else, there are plenty of scandals that have rocked the football world, but most of those have resulted in certain players being fined, or teams penalized."

Rumors of cheating and subsequent allegations went worldwide. Teams paid off refs; players had been paid off to influence the outcome of games. Many players had been publicly exposed for cheating of an entirely different sort when affairs they were involved in came to light. But which of those would result in three murders—two a decade-old—and another threat of the same?

"Check the records for players' deaths in the last fifteen years."

I ended the call and stood in the doorway of the bedroom where Ezzie slept, and studied her. How could I have been so daft to not have recognized her? And why hadn't she told me who she was besides a *Times* reporter? Why hadn't she reminded me of how we'd known each other as children?

I thought back on the few interactions we'd had. Somehow I'd found out that Esland and Darrow were friends, but I couldn't recall the exact conversation. Had there been a time when I let her get a word in edgewise, or had most of our interactions been like the one in the pub when I slung her over my shoulder and carried her out, refusing to listen to another word she said?

Esland rolled in her sleep, so I could see her face. She looked peaceful. Did that have to do with me, or was it this place that reminded her of a time spent here with her parents?

"What are you so deep in thought about?" she asked.

"You."

She held out her hand. "You were supposed to be next to me when I woke."

"My apologies," I said, dropping my trousers. I slid under the sheet and pulled her naked body against me.

"What were you thinking about specifically?"

"The memories you have of this place with your parents."

She smiled. "They're good ones. Although most of the memories of time spent with them are good."

"Was there a reason your father brought you here so often?"

"Wasn't my father. It was my mother."

"And her reason?"

"She grew up here. Lord Westbrook was her grandfather."

"Why didn't you say?" I gasped.

"By way of what? It isn't as though it's still a familial home."

"I'm sure anyone here would love to know you're Max's great-granddaughter."

Esland smiled. "You know of him?"

"Who in the UK doesn't?"

Lord Maxwell Westbrook was one of the most powerful men in twentieth-century England. He'd been a kingmaker, power broker, and by some accounts, major mischief maker. Most in England considered him the father of modern-day political publicism. Like Esland and her mother, Max was a newspaperman, eventually owning the *Daily Express* and its Sunday version. He could make or break almost anyone in politics via his papers. They were a tool he used to promote his friends as well as undermine his opponents.

"He was a cabinet minister, was he not?"

"That's right. During *both* World Wars. My mother once said that if Winston Churchill was Britain's bull-dog, then her grandfather was surely its bark."

"Journalism runs in your family."

"Reporters, even newspaper owners, don't have the power they used to. Maybe none ever had the power Max did. It's said that the guest book from his funeral reads like a who's who of the twentieth century."

"I saw when we came in that Churchill spent a great deal of time here."

"He did. So did H.G. Wells. I think the three were best mates—equally admired and feared." She shook her head. "My mother once told me Wells said that if my great-grandfather ever got to Heaven, he wouldn't last long."

"Why not?"

"The way I remember the story, Wells said something about him being chucked out for trying to merge Heaven and Hell after having secured a controlling interest in both places."

"Your mother went into journalism because of him?"

"Oh, yes. Although I think he was disappointed that she went the direction she did. She was more of a social reporter."

I remembered Esland mentioning that before.

"He'd be proud of you."

She turned so she was on her back and looked up at the ceiling. "God, I hope so. Although, if I don't do something to get justice for my parents' death, I fear they'll all be disappointed in me."

"That's a heavy weight to carry on your shoulders."

"No more than they carried. In fact, considerably less."

"Come on, let's go search out that tree house again," I said, attempting to lighten her mood.

"Must we?"

"I told you it's become imperative."

"I'd rather stay where we are."

"Okay."

Esland laughed. "That was far too easy."

"I don't care where we are. I just want to know you, Ezzie. Everything about you."

"Mildly daunting, Axel." She smiled, turned to her side, and propped her head on the hand of her bent arm.

"Tell me more about your father."

"The thing I remember most is how much he loved the game of football."

"It showed."

"He hated to lose, but winning for him was based on skill, performance, and hard work. The pressure on him was intense. I remember hearing him and my mother discuss his leaving Willingham Allied on more than one occasion when they thought I couldn't hear."

"That would've been a travesty." Graham Cartwright still held the scoring record not just for WA, but for all of the Master League.

"He'd had better offers, but it was never about the money; it was about the sport. And the team."

"Right," I murmured. "His loyalty to his club was one of the reasons fans adored him."

"He was a good man, Axel."

"I don't doubt it for a minute."

"He abhorred cheating of any kind."

"Do you think that's what he uncovered?"

"Of some nature, but what specifically, I don't know. There was a time…"

"What?"

"I remember him arguing with someone…he didn't know I'd come in. I'd never heard my father so angry."

"Any idea who it was?"

She closed her eyes and rubbed her temples. "I can hear his voice. There was something distinct about it." Her eyes sprang open. "Charlie Ambrose."

"Rumored to be a damn dirty player."

"Charlie had a lot of power in the league. Even more than my father."

"Why?" It wasn't as though he'd been one of the better players.

Esland shrugged. "I've no idea."

"Your father played for WA before Charlie did, right?"

She nodded. "I remember he fought against the trade. WA lost three good players for one not as good."

"Why did the club want him?"

"No idea." She closed her eyes like she had before and rubbed her temples.

"You've remembered something else."

"I'm not certain what though. There were other conversations. I didn't understand them at the time."

"Tell me what you do recall."

She took a deep breath and slowly blew it out. "One of the younger players came to him."

"You overheard them?"

"He talked about being pressured to 'join the program.' I remember him saying he knew my father wasn't part of it."

"What about Tommy Sholes? Do you remember any conversations between him and your father?"

Esland shook her head. "No, but…"

"What?"

"I'm trying to remember his name. He was a coach, but he hadn't been with the team very long."

"Pattison?"

"Yes, that's who it was. He came to the house several times. I remember my mother detested him."

"At that time, he'd just started as defensive coach."

"Now he's head coach."

I shook my head and closed my eyes. "Whatever was going on then, still is."

"What, though, and where is the proof?"

"It's hard to imagine that your father wasn't collecting it. Or your mother. She was a journalist after all, regardless of what kind."

Esland's eyes opened wide, and her skin paled.

"What is it?"

"My mother's diaries."

"Do you have them?"

"No, but I know where they are."

"Where?"

"Here."

20

Esland

It had been years since I fought off rainy-day boredom and had gone in search of Grandpa Max's archives and found my mother's diaries among them.

Reading them now made me look at my mother differently as a journalist. Many of the stories she'd written were hard-hitting, not the usual fluff that featured Veronica Cartwright's byline.

I wasn't certain there'd be anything in them about whatever my father had discovered about Willingham Allied or the league itself, but it was worth looking.

"Tell me where they are," Axel said, donning a jacket. "I'll go get them."

"You won't be able to. You won't be allowed in."

He took out the MI5 credentials I hadn't seen before. "Yes. I will."

I shook my head. "Those won't work."

"Care to wager?"

I laughed. "Sure, but I'll warn you, only family is permitted entrance into this particular part of the main house."

"Which means you'll have to divulge your affiliation."

He looked far too happy that I would. "Why does it matter to you?"

"It's your birthright, Ezzie. Your legacy isn't just from your father's lineage. In fact, your mother's is far more significant. It's something you should be proud of."

"I am proud. Very much so."

"And yet you keep it a secret. Why?"

Why did he have to be so perceptive? It made him good at his job, of course, but with me, it seemed like he immediately saw what everyone else overlooked.

"It's important to me that my byline is of my own merit, not due to whom I'm related."

He nodded as though that made sense to him. "It will open doors, in this case, a very important one."

He opened the passenger door for me, leaning forward to kiss me before I climbed in.

"We could've walked," I said, but it didn't seem as though he heard. "Axel?"

"Hmm?"

"Did you hear me?"

He nodded, but he appeared distracted. "I'll be right back," he said, getting out of the 4x4 and shutting the door behind him.

I watched as he went into the cottage only to come out a few seconds later.

"What are you about?" I asked when he returned to the vehicle and fastened his lap belt.

"I needed to check something."

"I see." I turned my head away.

"We aren't alone here, Ezzie."

"That shouldn't come as a surprise, but it does."

"They're here for your protection."

Fundamentally, I understood. Inexplicably, though, it bothered me. More interesting was how quickly Axel picked up on my discomfort and reassured me.

When I exited the 4x4 after Axel pulled up to the portico and opened my door, I looked about.

"You won't see them."

"I sense them, though. I'm not sure if it's because you planted the seed of their presence, or if it's instinctual."

"Always go with instinctual. If your gut is telling you something is off, listen, and then act."

"I understand."

"Do you?"

"I just said I did."

"There are times your intuition will go against what you believe to be true. You must be strong enough to toss your previous beliefs aside and protect yourself."

The somber sincerity of his words sent a chill up my spine. He saw something coming. He must; otherwise, why the serious nature of his warning?

The clerk behind the desk stood when we walked in, as though he'd expected us.

"Good afternoon," he said. "What may I do for you?"

"I need access to the archives," I said, prepared to issue proof of why it should be granted.

"Certainly," he said, pulling something from a drawer. "Follow me."

"Are these open to the public?" I tried to mask the horror in my voice at the idea.

"Under no circumstances," the man answered.

"But…"

"Miss Cartwright, you are hardly a stranger to Westbrook. Did you think for one moment you wouldn't be recognized?"

Out of the corner of my eye, I could swear I saw Pinch cringe. Was it because he hadn't recognized me himself?

The clerk stepped between Axel and me, who immediately pulled out his MI5 credentials.

"Miss?"

"His access is needed for an investigation into my parents' accident," I blurted. If there was ever a reason the rules should be eased, the death of a Westbrook family member should be more than sufficient.

"Certainly," the man repeated, stepping out of Axel's way.

When the clerk closed the door behind us, I walked straight over to the books I recognized as belonging to my mother.

"How do you want to approach this?" Axel asked.

"I should've thought to bring my trunk. It would make it easier to take these back to the Garden House."

"Not happening."

I set the diary I'd just taken off the shelf on a table. "What do you mean?"

"You—and the diaries—are safer here."

That made sense. If we were able to find anything significant in them, it may be the only lead we had.

Axel stood beside me. "Do you want my help, or would you rather do this on your own?"

"I don't know," I finally answered after contemplating his question.

"I'll be right here when you decide." He sat down at a table across the room, turned the chair around, and perused the volumes of hardbound books on the shelf.

"You're welcome to look at any of those," I said, immediately feeling silly for thinking he needed my permission.

Axel picked out one of the thicker volumes and brought it over to the table where I sat. "I decided I wanted to be closer to you."

"Maybe closer still would be better."

He smiled, spun the book around, and came to sit beside me. He laid his hand on mine where it rested on the first diary.

"I…"

He squeezed my fingers. "There's no hurry. We can postpone until tomorrow if seeing them here was enough for today."

When I leaned toward him, he wrapped his arm around my shoulders. "This is harder than I thought it would be," I whispered.

He lifted my chin and kissed me. When he backed away and looked into my eyes, I opened the first book. With him by my side, I could do this.

"It doesn't look as though they were shelved in any particular order," I said after thumbing through the first three I'd pulled out.

"Would it help if I tried to sort them?"

"It would."

We both stacked diaries on the table and began going through each of the piles, sticking a note on the front of each with the dates included in it. When I came to the one from the year before the accident, I sat down and began reading.

It was as though I were being transported back in time as I read the first entry.

The house is too quiet without the laughter of our sweet Ezzie. Even Graham seems to have lost his way without the presence of our beautiful daughter.

When my eyes filled with tears, Axel handed me a handkerchief and took the chair beside me. There were days scattered here and there without any entries at all, but most in the beginning were written in the weeks right after I left for university.

Graham has promised we'll spend the weekend in town with Ezzie. Hope she doesn't mind us infringing on her independence.

"Not quite so much their 'third to two who didn't need one,'" Axel murmured, stroking my cheek with his finger.

I smiled and continued reading. A little over an hour, and two diaries later, I came to what we'd been looking for, even though it was not what I could ever have predicted.

21

Pinch

"I've found something," Esland said, looking up and moving the diary between us. To this point, I'd tried my hardest not to read over her shoulder, but now I skimmed the open pages.

"It wasn't your father; it was your mother," I said when I got to the bottom of the entry.

"At first he didn't even realize she was conducting an investigation."

The pages that followed contained details of her mother's meetings with the UK's Football Governing Organization as well as the World Anti-Doping Agency.

"She went undercover for them," Ezzie gasped, awe evident in her voice.

I'd had a feeling the scandal related to doping. Paying off refs and players seemed passé. Even corruption within the International Football Governing Organization itself ceased to make front-page news.

Ezzie turned the page, and what I read there was so much worse than doping.

"Oh my God," she gasped, covering her mouth with her hand after reading the same passage I just had.

The organization is now exhaustively examining a number of reports of 'historically anomalous behaviors' of varying levels of gravity and connection to the club over a period spanning more than fifty years.

"Longer than that now."

"Good God," I muttered. Ezzie's mother had personally interviewed former professional footballers who had waived their rights to anonymity and agreed to talk publicly about being abused by former coaches and scouts in the seventies, eighties, and nineties.

What her mother had been investigating right before the accident, was to what extent the clubs had covered up these allegations.

"They just dropped it," Ezzie murmured, leaning back in her chair. "The league hired her, but after the accident, no further investigations were conducted."

I nodded. "That we know of."

"Right. But if countless former players spoke out about the abuse, why was there never a formal probe? We would've known of it. There's no way something of that nature could have been kept from the press."

My working theory was that initially the organization had wanted Esland's mother to find evidence of doping. When Veronica uncovered something exponentially more damaging, they shut it down. The allegations were likely never shared outside of UKFGO, which meant they probably never reported the evidence of doping she found either.

"It isn't just the league, Axel. It's the entire organization."

I agreed. There were more than 7,900 youth clubs in England alone. The idea that there had been an institutional cover-up or even a pedophile ring operating within the sport, turned my hardened stomach.

We sat in silence and continued to read and digest details of the countless interviews her mother had conducted with former and then-current players.

"Why didn't the players speak out?"

I sat back in my chair. "Payoffs?"

"Makes sense. A few million here or there to protect the billions of pounds the sport generates on an annual basis would be nothing to the organization."

Esland flipped through the diary's pages. "Look," she said, pointing to a name.

"Paulo Teska. What of him?"

"He retired back to Brazil after a few short years of lackluster performance. We ran a story about him and other players who ended their careers with inexplicable wealth. Paulo came from the depths of poverty, and yet now he's worth millions."

"What did the *Times* conclude?"

"The rumor was that he was paid to cover up *something*, but the paper had no proof of what specifically."

"Now we know."

"What do we do?"

I scrubbed my face with my hand, unsure how to respond. All I was certain of was that no matter the approach we decided on, Esland would be in far more danger than she was now.

Before our unplanned stop at Westbrook, it had been my intention to transport Ezzie out of the UK. Believing the threat against her came from Willingham Allied or the Master League, I'd naively thought hiding her in France would keep her safe. Now I knew that wouldn't be the case. But where could we go that she would be protected? Only one place came to mind.

"We have to leave, don't we?" she asked as though she were reading my mind.

I hated the sadness I heard in her voice. "Not today, but I do have some arrangements to make. Will you be okay on your own if I step out for a bit?"

Esland smiled. "I think I'll manage."

I leaned over and kissed her. "I'm proud of you, Ezzie."

"What have I done besides read through my mother's diaries?"

"Even as daunting as what we've discovered is, you have no intention of backing away from it."

"I don't. I couldn't. My parents lost their lives because of it."

"And that is why I'm proud of you."

"How are you managing with the fair maiden Esland?" Shiver said when he answered my call.

"We've stumbled upon something, Shiv, and it's big."

"I see." My friend's voice had gone from teasing to quite serious. "What can I do to help?"

It was the way of everyone in the Whittaker family. The first thing they typically did upon hearing of another's problems was to ask what they could do to help.

"If we pursue this—I don't see how we couldn't—the danger that Esland is in will become far worse. For her protection, I'd like to take her to America."

"That bad, eh?"

"Worse, Shiver. So much worse."

"I can arrange for private transport if that's what you're asking. Do you have a location in mind, or are you asking for that as well?"

"I intend to discuss it with Z."

"Good plan. Let him know that I can arrange for additional security once you're there."

"Thanks, Shiv."

"Of course. How soon can you be ready to leave?"

I sighed. I'd just told Ezzie we wouldn't have to leave today.

"You can come here for the night if you don't feel comfortable staying wherever you are. I'm certain I can put this into place by morning, at least the logistics of it."

"Again, thank you. It may take us until then to prepare the evidence for MI5 to collect."

"Right. I'll get back to you as soon as I'm able."

The next call I made was to Z, and it went much the same way as the call with Shiver had. By the time that call ended, my former boss had already made arrangements for a warrant to collect Veronica Cartwright's diaries once Esland and I were on our way to the States. In the meantime, Pique would stay on to ensure nothing was removed from the archive room between now and then.

"I'll get in touch with Quint and let him know you're bringing Esland to the ranch, unless you have somewhere else in mind."

"I was thinking of the ranch myself."

"Good, good," said Z. "I'll take care of it."

"There's one more thing we need to discuss: the DG position." I took a deep breath before continuing.

"I'll not make any kind of decision until this investigation is over with, if that's what's concerning you."

"I think you should."

"Bloody hell," muttered Z. "You're thinking of retiring, aren't you? Shiver, Wilder, Wren…now you? Soon we'll have no agents left."

"Not that you're jumping to conclusions."

"Tell me that isn't what you were going to say."

I laughed. "Not quite; however, I was going to suggest that George may be the better candidate for DG, given this case may take a while."

"I'll take it under consideration." Z sighed.

"We can discuss it further when I return."

"When will that be? Do you know?"

"As soon as you can arrange for someone to take over in Texas."

"Anyone you'd like to suggest?"

As much as I would've preferred anyone else, Pique was the best man for the job. He and Edge, and I told Z so.

Logic told me that Esland and Darrow were two very different women; however, knowing that my former girlfriend's affections had so easily been won over by another man, left me feeling somewhat insecure. Not that I'd admit it to a single other soul. It was hard enough to admit it to myself.

When I returned to the archive room, Esland was both pacing and chewing her fingernails.

"What else did you find?"

She handed me one of the diaries. "Read for yourself."

"Flipping heck," I muttered after I'd read what she pointed out. How could one sport be filled with so much corruption? It was a wonder the organization had

time to arrange for matches, given how much time they must spend cleaning up wrongdoings.

"The doping program appears to have rivaled that of the American cyclists," said Ezzie. "In fact, it's a toss-up as to which came first."

The doping allegations on their own would've been alarming, given the extent. However, up against the sexual abuse accusations, it paled greatly.

"Would you like to call it a day?" I asked, noticing her fatigue.

"I'd like to do more reading if you wouldn't mind. Perhaps one of her earlier volumes from before she got involved with the Football Governing Organization."

22

Esland

When Axel asked a second time whether I'd be okay on my own, I assured him I would. Before he left, he told me to let him know when I was finished at the main house, and he'd come and get me.

After another hour of reading, I was having as hard a time keeping my eyes open as I was hungry.

"Hello, Miss Cartwright," the clerk who'd greeted us earlier said when I came upstairs. "May I help you with anything?"

"I'd fancy some tea if it wouldn't be too much trouble."

"It would be my pleasure," the man answered.

"Wait, before you go, what is your name?"

"Hodges, miss."

"It's a pleasure to meet you, Hodges." I held out my hand, and we shook.

"If I may be so bold, you do look quite like your mum."

"Do I?" I didn't see it, personally. I didn't think I looked much like either my father or mother.

"Quite. She'd be so pleased that you're staying on here."

"Sadly, we must leave tomorrow. It was such a joy to be here again after so many years."

The man cleared his throat. "There is the matter of the trust to be discussed, as well as your intentions, miss."

"I've no idea what you're talking about."

"I believe the solicitor hoped to talk with you this afternoon if you were available. I told him you were visiting the archives."

"No one has said a word about a meeting." What was it Axel had told me? If my instincts were telling me something was wrong even when everything appeared on the up-and-up, to listen? Something about this didn't feel right.

"May I have the solicitor ring you?"

"Yes…no, wait." Axel had destroyed my mobile, which meant that there was no way for the solicitor to reach me directly, nor was there any way for me to reach Axel to tell him I was finished. "I'll get back to you on that. Best to skip the tea, Hodges, but thanks."

I put on my jacket and went out the front entryway of the main house. The walk to the cottage would do me good. Perhaps I could shake off some of the lingering effects of what I'd read about the footballers and the alleged sexual abuse.

At the same time, I had a lot to think about in regard to my mother. The woman I'd seen in the diaries today was vastly different than the perception I had of my mother when I was growing up.

For one, my mother certainly never saw me as a third wheel, not that it sounded as though my father had, either. Curious that I'd always believed they had.

Secondly, I'd never respected my mother as a journalist, because I'd believed she took the easy way out—reporting fluff rather than hard-hitting news. I couldn't have been more wrong in that regard. My mother was more of an investigative reporter than I could call myself.

The work she'd done on the football league would've changed the course of the sport in the UK and perhaps throughout the world. What had I done that would make an equal impact? Nothing.

"Fancied a walk alone?"

Pique was suddenly at my side, appearing out of nowhere. I startled. I nodded, not feeling comfortable explaining why I was, as he'd said, walking alone.

"Find anything of note today?"

"You should ask Axel. He's your boss, no?"

"Right. Well, enjoy the rest of your walk."

I thanked him, but the hair on the back of my neck stayed on end. Something about the man made me uncomfortable, and again, as Axel had said, I should always trust my instincts.

I looked up and saw the very man who'd given me the advice, walking in my direction, waving. Every nerve ending in my body went on high alert, and not in the way it had when Pique sneaked up on me.

The jumper he wore was tight across his chest, and the dungarees went taut on his thighs with every step he took toward me. His two-day stubble was looking more like a closely cropped beard today. He wasn't close enough for me to see the predominant color in his hazel eyes, but regardless, when they bored into mine, I could easily melt into a puddle at his feet.

He was smiling, which had first taken me some time to get used to. Prior to my coming to him for help, I didn't recall ever seeing Axel smile, except for when we were children.

"It just dawned on me that I didn't replace your mobile. I was on my way to fetch you."

"I didn't mind the walk."

"You should've had the clerk ring me."

"Would he have known your mobile number?"

"Right," he said, scrunching his eyes. "I'm sorry."

"Don't worry. The walk did me good…"

"But?"

"Nothing, really. Pique just struck up a conversation with me. I didn't see him approach."

"He fancies you," Axel said with a growly tone.

"I don't think so."

"Matters not. You're mine, and if he doesn't know it by now, I'll soon convince him in a way that leaves no question."

"Possessive, are we?" I laughed.

Axel put his arms around me and kissed me soundly, grabbing my arse with both hands.

Squealing and twisting away from him, I took his hand and pulled him toward the cottage.

"I need to replace your mobile. Please don't let me forget again."

"I've something else on my mind entirely, so you might have to remind me."

"What is on your mind, sweet Ezzie?" Axel asked, wiggling his brows.

I walked into the cottage and closed the door behind us. "As you know, I much prefer being unclothed. I'm hoping you're feeling the same way."

"Let me help you into your comfort zone," he said, pulling my blouse over my head.

When I was naked, I moved his hands so I could undress him.

Once naked like I was, Axel lifted my body into his arms and carried me into the bedroom.

"When this is over and we no longer need to have a security team in place, I vow to make love to you in every room of this cottage, not just the ones with draperies." Axel walked over and released the tie that held the curtains open. "Perhaps we'll even find your tree house and christen it."

I smiled. The man was so different than my impression of him. He was flirty and funny, playful and, oh, so sexy.

"We'll come back here when this is over?" I asked.

"For an extended holiday."

When he kissed me and covered my body with his, I put the conversation I'd had with the clerk about the solicitor out of my mind, hoping I remembered to bring it up to him later.

23

Pinch

"We'll have to leave tomorrow," I told her as Esland lay in my arms and I stroked her forehead. "I'd hoped we'd be able to stay another day or two, but I fear far too much for your safety."

"I told the clerk I thought we might have to leave this afternoon." Her hand drifted beneath the bedclothes, and my body stirred at her touch.

"You'll do me in, lass," I teased, kissing her forehead. We'd spent the last two hours sating one another's bodies, and while I'd never grow tired of feeling her naked beside me or burying myself deep in her warmth, I'd heard her stomach grumbling as much as mine.

"Would you like to stay in tonight or go to the main house? I noticed there was a menu for delivery."

"Oh, I'm glad you mentioned the main house. I had the oddest conversation with Hodges before I walked back. He said something about a solicitor needing to talk to me about…what was it he said? A trust."

She sat up, not bothering to pull the bedclothes over her nakedness. I'd not complain, but it might take me a bit to grow used to her unabashed need to be unclothed.

"Who is Hodges?"

"The clerk."

The idea that I hadn't learned the man's name was alarming. I seriously needed to get my head back in the game. I hoped Pique had done a once-over of the staff on his own since I hadn't asked him to see to it.

"What are your thoughts on his comment about the solicitor?"

"That is odd," I said, trying to steer my gaze away from her hardening nipples. Instead, I reached over and covered one breast with my hand and brought my mouth to the other. "Far too tempting."

When Esland's stomach grumbled a second time, I released her breasts and laughed. "I need to feed you."

"I'm okay," she said, snuggling up to me.

"You're not. You're starving, and since you're in my care, I must do my duty and see to it that you eat."

"And if I beg differently?"

"Your wish will be my command after dinner."

"Miss Cartwright, I was so pleased when Mr. Fulton rang to say that you'd be joining us for dinner. The solicitor—"

"I'm sorry, Hodges, but I don't know what a solicitor needs to speak with me about."

I rubbed her shoulder. "Whatever it is, can wait," I murmured; however, Hodges seemed to be growing increasingly agitated.

"Mr. Nicholas is waiting in the dining room, miss. Forgive me if I've overstepped, but the matter is quite urgent. He's been trying to reach you for some time, and the decision must be made prior to your thirtieth birthday. In fact, when you arrived, I thought that was why you were here."

Esland brought her hands to her head and rubbed her temples; I led her away from Hodges. "We'll be back," I said behind us as we walked away.

Once we were outside, under the portico, I took her hands in mine and held them tightly.

"We can handle this however you'd like. I can go in on my own and tell this Mr. Nicholas that you're unable to speak with him this evening. Or we can go in together, and you can get whatever it is dealt with now." I smiled and took a deep breath. "The final option is that you go in on your own, and I mind my own bloody business."

"I'd rather you were with me."

"Very well, then. Let's get this done. Whatever it is."

I saw Hodges wipe his brow when we came back inside and I motioned that we were ready to go into the dining room.

A portly gentleman, who appeared as distressed as poor Hodges, stood when we entered the room.

"Miss Cartwright," the man said, holding his hand out. "I'm Mr. Nicholas, and I'm the solicitor for your great-grandfather's trust."

I introduced myself and held the chair out for Esland to take a seat.

"This is a private matter," Mr. Nicholas leaned over and said to me when I pulled out a chair to sit as well.

"He stays or I don't," Esland told the man.

"Very well," Nicholas muttered, sitting down himself. "If we may begin, I don't intend to interrupt your dinner."

"Go ahead," said Esland, whose hands were folded on the table in front of her.

"As you are aware, Lord Westbrook owned this estate along with three other properties. When his daughter, your grandmother, passed, those properties were held in trust for your mother, as they are now for you."

"I'm sorry, *what*?"

"The properties are held in trust for you, Miss Cartwright."

"Yes, I heard you, but you began by saying as I'm aware. I assure you, I couldn't be less aware of what you're talking about."

"I see," he said, wiping his brow with his handkerchief and then stuffing it back in his jacket pocket. "I suppose, then, I should start at the beginning."

"Please," Esland responded.

I put my hand on her leg, and when I did, she dropped one of hers and grasped mine tightly.

"You see, the properties have all been provided for in terms of maintenance via the trust. Westbrook is the only one of the four that is on lease to the monarchy, which is merely a technicality. It's actually Parliament that oversees the estate and the income generated by the lease."

"Westbrook isn't privately held?" Esland asked.

"In a manner of speaking, it is held by the trust. The lease will expire on your thirtieth birthday, and a decision needs to be made as to whether you'd like to extend it. You are welcome to choose not to. As I said, the trust does allow for the maintenance of all four properties very generously."

"Was my mother aware of this?"

"Yes, miss. She elected to renew the lease indefinitely. The only thing prompting the renegotiation is that your mother passed, and this property, along with everything else in the trust, is scheduled to be distributed to you upon your thirtieth birthday which, if I'm not mistaken, is in a little more than a month's time."

"The first of March," Esland murmured.

Mr. Nicholas nodded and cleared his throat. "Have you not been receiving the correspondence I've sent?"

Esland's cheeks flushed, and she looked away from the solicitor. My guess was she hadn't paid the slightest bit of attention to the solicitor's letters and was now embarrassed of it.

"Miss Cartwright has had pressing matters causing her to be unable to respond to this point."

My sweet Ezzie smiled at me, and I winked at her.

"I see. Well, now that it's been presented to you, are you prepared to make a decision?"

"When, precisely, does this decision need to be made?" I asked on her behalf.

"Within two weeks of your thirtieth birthday," Mr. Nicholas said directly to Esland.

"There's time, then," she murmured.

"As I'm sure you can understand, this is a great deal to take in, given Miss Cartwright knew nothing of the trust's existence," I added.

"Certainly. I do have a prospectus for the four properties of which I've spoken, along with the details of the trust itself." He leaned over and pulled a leather satchel onto his lap. "I can leave this with you."

"Thank you," Esland responded, barely above a whisper.

"Please be in touch as soon as you've made a decision. My contact information is included. Keep in mind that regardless of your decision, there will be documents requiring your signature."

Esland nodded and stood when the solicitor did, as did I. Once the man was gone, we took our seats.

"I'm afraid I've lost my appetite," she said, staring over at the leather satchel rather than looking at me.

"Let's start with a drink and take it from there."

"I think I'll need more than a drink. Too bad you don't have any of your father's brandy."

"I do, at the cottage."

Esland laughed, and the sound was like music to my ears. "I should've expected you would."

I laughed too. "My only fear was that it would be confiscated when we crossed from Dover to Calais."

"Really?"

"No," I said, shaking my head.

"Is that where we're going, to Calais?"

"Not any longer."

The smile left her face. "Where are we going?"

"Can we speak of it later?" I asked, looking about the crowded dining room.

"Of course. I'm sorry."

"Don't be," I said, stroking her cheek with my finger.

"I'd no idea," she murmured, her eyes once again settling on the satchel.

I opened one of the menus sitting on the table and handed it to her. "Tell me what sounds good, and we'll have it delivered to the cottage."

Her eyes lit up. "Are you certain?"

"That's where Wellie's brandy is, after all."

"Thank you, Axel."

"Of course. Be sure to look at the pudding menu as well, Lady Cartwright."

When she stuck her tongue out at me, I wanted to lean over and kiss her, but I'd wait until we were alone. Thinking of Esland's propensity for nudity and how soon we'd both be out of our clothes, I felt my trousers tighten.

"I'm so pleased you were able to meet with Mr. Nicholas," Hodges said as we were leaving.

"Thank you," murmured Esland.

When we returned to the cottage, I planned to take a moment to contact Pique and ask him to do a thorough background check on all of the staff at Westbrook. The idea that the solicitor had learned of Ezzie's presence from the desk clerk didn't sit right with me. Neither did the idea that Hodges appeared to be well aware of the trust.

"Dinner will be delivered shortly," Hodges said when we walked out the door to the portico where the 4x4 was waiting.

On the ride back, Esland looked out the window into the darkness. "What's on your mind, sweetness?" I asked, reaching for her hand.

"Remember when you told me that even in the face of logic, I should trust my instincts?"

"Of course I do."

"When Hodges first mentioned that a solicitor wanted to meet with me, something didn't feel right."

I nodded, murmuring my agreement.

"Why did I know nothing of this? There was nothing whatsoever about it in any of my parents' documents."

"It is a mystery. Particularly that your mother didn't leave anything about it for you. What about in her will?"

"She didn't have one. Neither did my father."

"But you did inherit?"

"Of course. I was their sole heir."

I wondered if my father had a will. Not that he had much to leave me, and not that I cared about whether he did or not. The point was more that I was a thirty-three-year-old man, and hadn't updated my will since I joined MI5 and it had been mandatory. The fact that Esland's parents hadn't left one, served as a reminder that I needed to see to it. I was a far wealthier man now than I'd been back then.

"It's a lesson. Particularly for you now."

Esland looked at me with wide eyes. "What would come of it, Axel? If something were to happen to me?"

"I can't answer that. You said both of your parents were only children." I reached over and pulled her hand away from her mouth and held it in mine.

"Where are we going, Axel?"

"The safest place I can think of now, Ezzie, is in America."

"I was hoping that was where you'd say."

"Were you also hoping I'd say that we're going to a ranch in Texas?"

She smiled. "Where Darrow ran off to?"

"Z assures me it's equally as safe as Whittaker Abbey. In fact, he'd probably attest that it's safer."

"A pissing match over security."

I laughed. "There is an abundance of that in our circle, isn't there? It gets worse if you include the K19 crew."

"The K19 crew?"

"Friends of Shiver's. Former military and CIA agents who now do private work."

"Black ops?"

"Something like that."

"Are they in Texas as well?"

"I'm sure they're wherever they need to be."

"I can't say that I'm anxious to meet them."

"No?" I laughed. Honestly, I couldn't say I'd be anxious for her to meet them either.

I parked the 4x4 and went around to open Esland's door. There'd never been a time in my life when I could remember being insecure about much of anything. Yet the idea of Esland being pursued by anyone other than me, left me feeling that way.

"What is it?" she asked, getting out of the vehicle but remaining between it and me.

I grasped her neck and brought my lips to hers. "You're mine, Ezzie. All mine. Do you understand me?"

"I think I've always been, Axel. What about you? Are you mine?"

"As long as you'll have me."

"And if I said I wanted you forever?"

"Then we'd want the same thing."

"Don't tease."

I lowered my mouth to hers and kissed her deeply. "Come inside with me, and I'll show how very serious I am."

She took my hand and pulled me toward the door.

"After we eat, however."

"Spoilsport," she said, sticking her tongue out at me like she had earlier.

"Come here," I groaned, pulling her body into mine. "Give me that tongue." I thrust mine into her mouth, tangling with hers, and brought both hands to her breasts, forcing her back against the wall of the entryway.

"You're wearing far too many clothes, Ezzie."

"As are you."

She wiggled out of my grasp, shedding layers as she ran toward the bedroom. I followed, doing the same.

24

Esland

"Oh my God. Isn't it divine?" I said, taking another bite of the grilled veal chop Axel had ordered. It was served with rosemary and lemon gremolata and cooked the perfect medium rare.

He nodded and smiled, moving his plate in front of me, and mine in front of him. "As is the crispy duck. It's one of my favorites, in fact."

"You're just saying that so I don't feel so badly about pinching your dinner."

"That's where it came from."

"I'm sorry, what came from?"

"My code name. Wilder took to calling me Pinch after my father caught me attempting to steal a candy from the market. You'd think I was trying to steal the crown jewels the way he went on about it. Never tried to steal again, though."

"That isn't quite as interesting a story as I imagined, Axel. Or that you led me to believe. However, I am sorry I stole your dinner."

"It's okay; I gave it gladly. Just don't get any ideas about my pudding."

He'd ordered a caramelized Sicilian lemon tart with poached clementines, which did sound fantastic. But my favorite from when my parents and I used to visit was the vanilla and cinnamon poached pears served with milk gelato. I'd never had anything like it anywhere else.

"Axel?"

"Yes, Ezzie," he said between mouthfuls of duck.

"I'm not sure how to say this."

"Out with it, then."

"Will you be staying on in America with me?"

He rested his fork on his plate, leaned forward, and looked into my eyes. "As long as I can. However, I'll need to return to the UK in order to investigate all that we found in your mother's diaries."

"I'll be staying on there."

"That's right."

I got up from the table and walked over to the window. Tommy Sholes' words echoed in my head. *Your father would want you to finish what he started.*

Tommy hadn't known that it was really my mother's work I would be finishing, but that didn't matter.

Both of my parents had been murdered, and I had no intention of taking a step back and letting anyone else solve the crime.

"I'm a journalist, Axel. How will I be able to assist with the investigation if I'm in America and you're here?"

"You won't," he said without fanfare or apology.

"But—"

"It isn't up for discussion, Esland. Your life was threatened, and I'll keep you as far from danger as I can."

I spun around on him, arms folded. "It isn't your decision alone."

He stood and walked over to me, tugging on my arms until I dropped them. "The investigation has been taken over by MI5. They'll collect the evidence from the archives here at Westbrook and deliver it to head-quarters. In the meantime, other agents will be working diligently to collect more from every other source they can, including scheduling interviews with the victims your mother spoke with twelve years ago. All the while, whoever murdered your parents, as well as Tommy Sholes and who knows how many others, will be doing everything in their power to thwart our progress, including committing additional murders."

"You will be in danger equal to me."

"It's different."

I walked into the entryway, picked up my clothes, and pulled on my knickers followed by my bra.

"What are you doing?" Axel asked.

"What's it look like? I'm getting dressed."

"Where are you going?"

"I'm not going anywhere. I just don't want to be naked around you right now."

"That makes no sense. Don't do this, Ezzie. You came to me for help; now let me help you."

"You're right. I did come to you for help. Help, Axel. Not for you to tuck me in a wardrobe somewhere to wait while you solve the crimes I should be by your side, investigating."

"I disagree."

"Of course you do. Good night, Axel."

"Wait. What about the pudding?"

"You can have it. This time I really have lost my appetite."

I walked down the hallway to a room that neither of us had occupied, went inside, and closed the door, locking it behind me.

When I felt myself drifting to sleep an hour later, I wasn't sure if I was glad or disappointed that Axel hadn't come looking for me.

"Ezzie, open the bloody door!" I heard Axel shouting, and sat straight up in bed. Was it real, or was I dreaming? I ran to the door.

"What's happened?" I gasped.

"I could hear you from down the hall. You were having a nightmare."

I ran my hand through my hair. What I remembered of my dream was quickly dissipating. All I knew was that someone had had me in their grasp and were threatening to kill me. Worse, in my dream, Axel lay dead on the pavement.

He wrapped his arms around me and kissed my forehead. "Let's not do this, please."

"Do what?"

"You shut me out."

I turned toward the bed. "You're shutting me out, Axel. There's no difference."

"Which is why I said let's not do this."

"What does that mean, exactly?"

"It means that I don't want to keep repeating mistakes I've made in the past. Especially with you. It means we talk about it, and we compromise. Both of us."

"I won't allow you—"

Before I could finish, he kissed me. I wrapped my arms around his neck, kissing him back harder. Axel put his hands on my arse, lifted me, and I wrapped my legs around him, pressing my sex against his hardness. With our mouths still fused together, he carried me down the hallway to the bed we'd shared the night before.

"We'll figure this out, Ezzie. I promise."

I rested my head on the pillow and watched as he removed my clothes first, before taking off his trousers and laying his naked body against mine.

"I need you in my life, sweetness. I understand how you're feeling; I swear on my father's life I do. It's just, the idea that something could happen to you is more than I can bear to think about."

"I feel the same way." I put my fingertips on his lips. "Let's not talk anymore now, Axel. Please just love me."

He slid down my body and settled between my legs. I groaned, winding my fingers in his hair. The pleasure was so intense I couldn't think whether to keep him where he was, or pull him away. Axel grasped my hips, taking the decision away from me.

"Come for me, Ezzie."

I arched my back and let the orgasm take over my mind and body. When I felt as though I was about to come back down to earth, Axel thrust inside me, bringing me right back to the brink of ecstasy.

"You're mine," I heard him growl through the haze of yet another orgasm. This time when I went over the precipice, Axel came along.

He rolled to my side and cupped my cheek. "I can't bear arguing with you, nor can I stand it, knowing you're in bed a few feet from me instead of with me where I can feel your naked body next to mine."

"I feel the same way, Axel. Honestly, I do, but—"

"Shh," he whispered. "I made you a promise, and I intend to keep it."

25

Pinch

I wrapped my arm around Esland, who was fast asleep with her head on my chest. Sleep for me would not come easy. I told her we'd figure it out, and because of that promise, I had a lot of thinking to do.

Initially, I'd planned to travel to the States with Esland, get her settled, and ensure her safety. Once I had, my intention was to return to the UK and take up the investigation of the Football Governing Organization.

Z gave me the authority to put a team together, and I'd already begun considering who I'd employ on it. I'd have Pique stay in America with Esland, and perhaps either Edge or Grinder. The rest of her security team could be contracted with the help of Shiver's contacts at K19 Security Solutions. While they were based on the coast of California, my understanding was K19 had operatives all over the US.

That had been my plan before I promised Esland we'd figure it out together. Leaving her blanketed in protection would've allowed me to focus on the case and solve it far faster than I would distracted. If that was the way I handled it, though, I would lose my sweet Ezzie forever, and I couldn't allow that to happen. I loved her, and whether she was ready to hear the words from me didn't matter; it was the way I felt, and nothing would ever change it.

"No," Ezzie groaned. "It can't possibly be morning already." I looked down at her opened eyes.

"I'm afraid it is, but it's far too early for either of us to be awake. Go back to sleep, sweetness."

"You're awake. In fact, you haven't slept all night." I smiled. "And you know this how?"

"Every time I opened my eyes, yours were too, and you were far too distracted to even notice me watching."

I angled my head to kiss her. "I'm sorry, Ezzie."

She kissed me and closed her eyes. Within a few seconds, her breathing had evened out. Thankfully, given I still didn't have a single clue how to handle the next few days. Instead of agonizing further, I closed my eyes as well and slept.

When I woke again, it was almost noon. There were likely messages from both Shiver and Z, regarding our travel plans. I eased Esland off my chest, slid out of bed, and went into the kitchen to check my voicemail.

As I'd expected, there were messages from both, along with one from Quint and another from Pique. I'd wait until later to call everyone back except Shiver. The man had pulled strings to make travel arrangements on my behalf. I owed him an immediate call return.

"Good afternoon," Shiver answered. "Late night?"

"Lot on my mind, Shiv."

"Yes, I would imagine. Listen, before we get deep into your travel schedule, I want you to know that I received a call from JohnTwo earlier this morning."

"Is everything okay with Darrow's training?"

"Yes, I believe it is, since he's volunteered her services."

"In what way?"

"To serve on your team."

"I see. Shall I thank Z after this call?" I groaned.

"Don't underestimate her, Pinch. Pope never would've made the offer if Darrow weren't ready."

"I'll think it over." Neither regard thrilled me—as additional protection for Esland nor as an investigator—but I wouldn't say so to Shiver.

Before ending our call, he informed me he'd made arrangements with the K19 Security team for transport, given the short notice.

"You'll stay the night at the abbey, connect with Darrow, and leave first thing tomorrow morning."

"Has the cost been approved?"

"Yes," Shiver answered, but I sensed hesitancy in his voice. In all likelihood, he was shouldering this expense on his own.

"There's something else I'd like to forewarn you about if we'll be at Whittaker Abbey this evening."

I told Shiver about the meeting Esland had with the solicitor.

"All the more reason to get her out of the bloody UK."

"Why so?"

"I'll explain more when you arrive."

"It may be easier now, Shiv, given she's still sleeping." I peeked into the room to confirm she was.

"There will be time tonight once Darrow arrives. You know the two will be thick as thieves for hours."

Not if I had anything to say about it. Selfishly, I had no intention of sharing Esland a minute more than I absolutely had to, and I didn't care whether Darrow liked it or not.

Without bothering to listen to Pique's message, or return Z's or Quint's calls, I climbed into bed with my sleeping beauty.

God knew what kind of privacy we'd have once we were in Texas. I was already concerned about Pique and Quint. Adding Darrow to the mix might mean we rarely had time on our own. I hadn't given Shiver an idea of when we'd arrive, which meant I had all afternoon to get lost in Ezzie's scrumptious body.

I opened the kitchen door to find the same basket we'd received previous mornings waiting inside the back porch. The pastries were no longer warm given it was afternoon, but that wouldn't take away from their deliciousness. I removed them the same way Esland had, turned the fire on under the tea kettle, and found a tray in one of the pantries.

"What are you about this morning?"

I turned to see the glorious nakedness of the woman who had so quickly captured my heart, illuminated by the sun's rays.

"'Tis afternoon, sweetness, but to answer your question, I was about to serve you breakfast in bed."

"You'll spoil me," she said, walking over to wrap her arms around my waist.

"Damn, you feel good," I said, pulling her body flush with mine. I cupped her cheek and looked into her eyes. "There's something I need to say to you, Esland. I fear that when I do, you'll think I've gone mad."

She scrunched her eyes. "Out with it," she whispered.

I looked up at the ceiling. "Now that I've begun, I suppose I must continue."

Esland tried to escape my grasp. "You needn't if you've changed your mind."

"I haven't, and I promise you, I never will."

"Axel, what is it?"

"Look at me, sweetness." When she did, I took a deep breath. "I'd tell you that I believe I'm falling in love with you, but the truth is, I've already fallen. Quite hard, in fact."

"You have?"

"Yes. I have."

"As have I, although to be perfectly honest, I believe I've loved you most of my life."

"That love is the reason I fear so much for your safety. I want you to understand that my desire to keep you thus is born solely of that. There is no other reason."

She smiled. "Not because you're trying to keep the pesky *Times* reporter out from underfoot?"

"I have been quite a wanker where you're concerned, haven't I?"

"No comment."

"Off the record?"

"Then, yes. Quite the wanker."

"Can you forgive me?"

"Long since forgiven, Axel."

I would give anything to be able to take the weight of this off her shoulders. Sadly, an investigation of this nature could take months, if not longer. How in the name of God would I be able to keep her out of harm's way for that amount of time if she insisted on working with me? Maybe having Darrow with us would help more than I'd initially thought. Perhaps she'd be able to convince Esland to let me handle the case while they stayed behind in Texas.

"That doesn't mean you're allowed free rein now, Axel. Whatever it is you're thinking, I suggest you reconsider before it's too late."

"Bloody heck," I muttered when she stomped off in the direction of the bedroom. This time I was on her heels, determined not to let her lock me out a second time.

26

Esland

"There is more we need to discuss, Esland," Axel said, following me into the bedroom.

How could a conversation in which the man of my dreams told me he loved me take such a terrible turn for the worse?

"What else?" I asked, turning to him with folded arms.

"We'll be staying at the abbey tonight and leaving for America in the morning."

"And then, what, Axel?"

"There will be a team traveling with us."

"Who is on the team?"

"Pique, Edge, and someone else you know quite well."

"I'm in no mood for teasing," I said, turning my back on him.

"Darrow will be traveling with us."

"What?" I asked, spinning around.

"I spoke with Shiver earlier. My guess is that either he or Z had a hand in her training officer offering her services."

"How does she feel about this *assignment*?"

"To be honest, I've no idea. Although I doubt that JohnTwo would volunteer her against her will."

"JohnTwo?"

"Sorry. General Pope. There's more."

"Go on, then."

"Shiver has made arrangements for the K19 Security team I mentioned previously to transport us."

"I see."

Axel walked over and pulled my arms from my body and put them around his waist.

"Do I have any say at all?" I asked.

"Always."

I raised a brow. "Very well, then. I don't care for Pique."

Axel scrubbed his face with one hand while he kept the other wrapped around my waist. "That gets complicated, Esland."

"You told me to trust my instincts, did you not? Even in the face of logic?"

"I did do."

"I don't like him. What's more, he makes me very uncomfortable. And if you recall, it was only a few short days ago that you questioned his actions."

"You're right. And as promised, we'll figure this out together, which means that I'll arrange for Pique's replacement when we get to the abbey."

"Thank you, Axel." I smiled and kissed his cheek. "I know that wasn't easy for you."

He raised a brow. "By way of what, sweetness?"

"By way of compromise, my love."

It hadn't occurred to me that Pique would be traveling to the abbey with us. It seemed that perhaps it hadn't occurred to Axel either; otherwise, he may have made different arrangements.

Axel and I were in the back seat of the 4x4 while Pique drove and Edge sat in the front passenger seat, like we had been when we rode from the pub to the Cotswolds. That seemed like weeks ago. Then, Axel loathed me; now, he loved me. Could that really be possible?

I felt his hand cover mine, and I looked over at him. His eyes scrunched in question, but this wasn't the time or place to discuss my doubt of him.

"What is the schedule tomorrow, boss?" asked Edge.

Axel took a silent deep breath and let it out. "You'll travel with us to the States. Pique, Rile, and Grinder will stay here."

From where I sat, I could see Pique's jaw tighten. Could Axel see it too?

"Are we off the case, then?" Pique asked.

Axel squeezed my hand.

"That will be up to Z."

While moments ago, Pique appeared tense, now he was agitated.

"I thought MI5 was handling the case."

"We are."

Edge turned his head and made eye contact with Axel, who shook his head.

No one spoke the rest of the drive, but at least two of the vehicle's occupants were seething. The tension unnerved me, and I couldn't wait to get out of the 4x4. I was likely not the only one who felt that way.

What I found interesting was that Axel didn't mention that Darrow was a planned part of the team traveling to the States. Perhaps that would've enraged Pique even more. Although from my perspective, the real work would be done here. It was curious he didn't see it that way.

With every mile we traveled closer to Whittaker Abbey, I felt my anxiety dissipate. It had always been that way when I visited as a young girl. In fact, the only time I remembered being trepidatious was the last time, when I'd believed I was bringing danger to the family's doorstep.

It wasn't as if it was different now, though. Danger traveled with me, which meant it was headed straight in their direction. Perhaps knowing it was the duke's idea that we stay the night at the abbey lessened my anxiety over doing so.

I sighed when we reached the gate, and Axel smiled.

"I'd like to stop in and visit my father before it gets much later. I'll have Pique drop you at the abbey."

"Would I be intruding if I went with you?"

"Not at all. In fact, I think he'd enjoy the visit."

Pique nodded that he'd heard us and took the turnoff that led to the cottages.

I wondered what had happened to Axel's mother. All I knew from Darrow was that she'd passed away when Axel was still very young. We were alike in that way, although my mother had lived until I was a young adult. I envied the close relationship he had with his father.

He came around and opened my door when we arrived, but I didn't hear him say a word to Pique or Edge.

"Where will they go?" I asked once the door was shut behind me.

"Edge will make arrangements for Pique to get transport back to London, and then he'll come here to collect us."

"Pique seems…piqued." I smiled and Axel did too.

"Apropos."

"There's a beautiful woman," said Axel's father when we stepped in the front door.

"Hello, Pops," said Axel, hugging him. "This is Esland Cartwright."

"I remember you, lass."

"How are you, Mr. Fulton?"

"Now, now, call me Wellie. Everyone does."

"Right. How are you, Wellie? I understand you were quite ill."

"Better now, although I think everyone made more of a fuss than was necessary."

Out of the corner of my eye, I could see Axel's face and the evident love he had for his father. He was so different from the man I'd believed him to be only a few days ago.

He was far softer-hearted, laughed more easily, and was so much less intimidating than I'd always believed him to be.

"Let's sit, but first, what can I get the two of you?"

"I can get whatever we need, Pops. You and Esland sit by the fire."

I followed Wellie but stopped when I noticed the photograph of Axel with my father that sat on the bookshelf. I picked it up. "I remember this day."

"One of my best memories," said Axel. "Looking at it the other day only filled me with remorse that I didn't realize you were Graham's daughter and that my good fortune in meeting him was all due to your benevolence."

"You give me too much credit. 'Twas Darrow that begged me to arrange for tickets to the match."

I caught Wellie's smiling gaze from the corner of my eye and turned to smile back at him.

"Fancy a brandy?" Axel asked.

"Please. I'm quite addicted to it," I said directly to Wellie, who smiled more broadly.

When Axel joined us, I took a seat, and he sat beside me after handing his father a glass.

"I told Pops that his brandy wasn't always the answer to every dilemma, but he informed me it only aided in finding them more easily."

"Quite," I agreed, taking a sip.

"We're leaving for the States in the morning, Pops."

Wellie nodded, and I wondered if Axel ever told him about the things he was investigating. That he didn't ask why, meant that they probably didn't discuss the specifics of whatever he was working on as it happened. Something told me that if he could, Axel would get great counsel from his father.

Wellie's eyes scrunched as he studied his son. Axel noticed and nodded.

"Was a tragedy, that accident," Wellie said, looking directly at me. "My heart broke for you at the time, lass."

"Thank you, sir," I whispered, my eyes filling with tears. My parents had been gone for almost twelve years, and while I missed them every day, I rarely got emotional when someone spoke of them.

"Axel tells me that there's a theory it wasn't an accident after all."

That answered my earlier question as to whether Axel confided in his father; he obviously did, at least in this instance.

I looked at Axel like his father had, and got a nod as well, which made me smile.

"I've recently learned that my mother was investigating a scandal involving Willingham Allied as well as the rest of the Master League, even the Football Governing Organization itself."

"Ah, so not your father so much as her." Wellie brushed his lower lip with his finger. "Although he likely made her aware of the scandal in the first place."

"Yes." I hadn't considered that was why or how my mother got involved, although it was an obvious supposition.

"It is much worse than we initially theorized, Pops."

"How so?"

"Sexual abuse within the league with the younger players. Coaches and the like."

Wellie grimaced. "Your dear mother and I argued heatedly about the abuse some suffered at the hands of the priests, and this was years and years before the scandal came to light."

"Are you Catholic?" I asked.

"No, but she was. When she was with child"—he pointed at Axel—"the debates we had about whether he would be raised in the church were extensive. Worst arguments we ever had."

"That is why we never attended services."

"After she passed, I couldn't bear the hypocrisy of involving you in any organized religion. What was to say that Protestant clergy didn't abuse children in the same manner?" Wellie shook his head. "Predators are not exclusive to any one religion or religion itself. They use any means they can to find their prey."

The sadness in his voice mirrored what I felt in my heart. To think that boys, and perhaps girls, looked to these men as role models, only to have their lives destroyed, saddened me as much as it made me feel ill.

"Darrow will be traveling with us," said Axel, perhaps in an attempt to steer the conversation in a different direction.

"She visited earlier. Quite excited, in fact, to realize her dream of serving Her Majesty."

"At our slumbers, she would say that one day she'd be the female equivalent of James Bond, while I fancied myself the next...well, it isn't important who; I just always aspired to be a crack newspaper reporter." The idea that the woman who was my childhood heroine had been shot dead outside my flat due to her pursuit of a story, hit too close to home for me to say aloud.

"I never knew that about Darrow. I believed it to be more of a recent aspiration," commented Axel. "Did you, Pops?"

Wellie shook his head. "Not that I recall."

I found that interesting. Was I the only one Darrow had confided in about it? That somehow made me love her even more.

"She'll be anxious to see you," Wellie spoke directly to me. "I'm surprised she hasn't knocked the door down. She was in quite a tizzy over your arrival when I saw her earlier."

"I should deliver Esland to the abbey," Axel said to his father. "We'll be leaving quite early tomorrow."

Wellie nodded and stood. It appeared to me that was no easy task.

Axel approached his father, and they hugged. "I love you, Pops," he said.

"And I, you," Wellie answered.

The scene almost brought tears to my eyes. Again, Axel surprised me.

"Come and give your future father-in-law a hug," Wellie said, winking.

"Pops," groaned Axel, sounding a bit like a teenage boy.

"What? Tell me I'm wrong."

Axel shook his head and laughed. "Perhaps a bit premature."

"Mark my words," Wellie said to me when we embraced.

While I was embarrassed, the truth was, nothing would bring me greater happiness than to one day be Axel's wife.

27

Pinch

"I'd apologize for my father's words, but I find myself hoping he's right," I said once we stepped out of the cottage and walked toward the waiting 4x4.

"Me too," said Esland, barely above a whisper.

When her cheeks flushed, I couldn't help myself. I kissed her.

"You never cease to surprise me, Axel Fulton."

"In what way do I surprise you?"

Esland shrugged. "You're just so different than I thought."

The remorse I felt wasn't limited solely to not realizing that I'd known her as a child. My recent treatment of her pained me greatly. "I'm sorry," I said for what felt like the umpteenth time, but no matter how often I said it, it didn't serve to diminish my regret.

"Let yourself off the hook, Axel," she said, patting my cheek and then kissing it. "I've forgiven you; you should do the same."

I growled deep in my throat and nuzzled her neck. "I'll spend tonight and every day and night that follows making it up to you."

"That, I'll accept." She smiled and pulled me toward the waiting vehicle. "It's freezing out here, Axel. Take me to the abbey and warm me."

Darrow, as was somewhat expected, came flying out of the abbey's entry when we drove up.

"True!" she exclaimed, rushing forward to hug her.

When she led Esland inside, I held back to talk with Edge. "Is there anything I need to know?"

Edge let out a deep breath. "I am equally perplexed. It's as though Pique has had a change in personality."

"Agreed, and I am skeptical that it is solely due to his previously believed attraction to Miss Cartwright."

"There's something else up with him, but I've no idea what it might be."

"I'm going to ask Z to reassign him."

"I'd do the same," admitted Edge. "Rough, though. We've worked together since the beginning of our careers."

"Me as well. However, until we can figure out why he's reacting as he is, I don't feel comfortable having him remain on this investigation."

"Who will you put in his place?"

"I've not decided yet. Although, it makes the most sense to have George take the lead until I return."

Edge nodded but appeared chagrined.

"There should be no sides here. We all work for Her Majesty, no matter what the stated position."

"I'll not apologize for my bias, Pinch. I'd like to see you named DG above her, and that has nothing to do with her being a woman."

I smiled inwardly. It didn't? Interesting in that I'd not said a word about gender.

"Will you be staying over at Dorchester House?" Edge asked.

"Not tonight," I snapped and then softened my expression. "No commentary necessary."

"I'll be at the abbey at zero five hundred."

"Very well."

Shiver met me when I came in the front door. "If you're looking, they're in the kitchen with Mrs. Mollybock," he announced. "And hello, Pinch."

Shiver's wife was behind him, holding their daughter, who surprisingly reached her hands out to me.

"You don't have to take her," said Losha.

I held out my hands, and the baby scrambled into my arms, resting her head on my chest.

"Bugger me," muttered Shiv, to which Losha smacked his arm. "Sorry, but look at them, she doesn't come as easily to me," he added.

Even I had to admit I wasn't typically someone babies or even little children paid any attention to and vice versa. I'd been known to play a rousing round of dragons and sorcerers with Shiv and Losha's son, Kazmir, but otherwise, wee ones and I ignored one another.

"Look at that," said Darrow, walking toward us with Esland following.

"What?" I heard my sweet Ezzie ask.

"Axel has Lilliya in his arms. He must be practicing for when the two of you have children."

Part of me wanted to wring Darrow's sarcastic neck, but when I saw the smile on Ezzie's face, I forgot the other woman entirely.

She approached and held a finger out, which Lilliya quickly grasped. Soon the baby was holding her arms out to Esland like she had to me.

"The two of you are disgustingly adorable," Darrow commented, but by her grin, I knew she didn't begrudge us, and for that, I was thankful.

I'd obviously not given her appropriate credit for how she'd handle me moving on with another woman. I should've realized, though, that she had been the first to move on.

Later, when we didn't have an audience, I'd ask whether she was comfortable with this detail, given we would be staying on the ranch with Quint. As with my previous relationship with the woman, it was impossible to know what the status of Darrow and the Texan's relationship might be.

"She's beautiful," I heard Esland murmur.

"As are you," I whispered, putting my arm around her shoulders.

"If you weren't leaving tomorrow, I'd employ both of you as child-minders," commented Losha, who now held a very heavy-looking Kazmir in her arms. "You remember Pinch," I heard her say to the little boy. "And the woman holding your sister is Miss Esland."

"Hello, Miss Esland," Kazmir said politely.

"I've dinner on the table," said Mrs. Mollybock, coming out from the main dining room. "Will it be just the five of you, then? I'd planned for seven."

I hadn't thought of inviting Edge, and that shamed me. "Six, if you'd be so kind."

"What of your father?" she asked.

"Flipping heck," I muttered. Had I no manners whatsoever? On the other hand, this was Shiver and Losha's house, and I had no business inviting extra dinner guests.

"Wellie begged off, Mrs. Mollybock, but Mr. Edgemon should be arriving shortly," Shiver told her.

"Edgemon?" whispered Esland.

I laughed. "His code name isn't terribly clever, is it?"

I held back while the ladies went into the main dining room.

"I've come to realize if Mrs. Mollybock had her druthers, she'd have named any other bloke in the United Kingdom Duke of Bedfordshire," said Shiver, standing beside me.

"I was wondering why she was asking me about your dinner guests."

"Losha has even spoken to her about it, but not because I asked her to."

"Perhaps my father would know what's behind it."

"Do me the courtesy of not embarrassing me by asking." Shiver squeezed my shoulder, smiled, and motioned for me to follow him to the table.

The look on Shiver's face when he sat next to his wife mirrored the way I felt when I took the open chair next to Esland. Shiv had taken a lot of Mickey, mainly from Wilder and me, about how he'd gone from a badass MI6 agent to a lovesick puppy when he finally convinced Losha, an equally badass former Russian assassin, to marry him.

Perhaps that was one secret to it. Esland impressed me in ways previously unimaginable. While I'd found her job as a reporter annoying before, now it filled me with pride. I supposed that had as much to do with the fact I wasn't working on a case for her to muck up by getting in the middle of.

"I'd like to begin by making a toast to my sister," Shiver said, standing with glass in hand. "I've never been prouder of you, Darrow. I may be retired; however, I will still welcome you to Her Majesty's Service."

I looked over at Darrow, the woman I'd love forever, but not in the way I'd once thought. I was equally proud of her, as I was certain Wilder would be when he heard how well her training had gone.

"I don't recall getting an assignment in the midst of training," Shiver said, looking between Edge, who had taken a seat during the toast, and me. "What about the two of you?"

"I barely made it through training," Edge said, laughing at himself. "Congratulations, Darrow."

"I'm not entirely finished. Once I've completed my current assignment, JohnTwo has called for my return to Fort Monckton."

"There is another possibility," said Shiver, brushing his lower lip with his finger.

It was another trait the Whittakers and I had picked up from my father. Whenever he was deep in thought, he did the same thing.

"Do tell, Thornton," said Darrow, leaning forward.

"You could continue training in the US."

"More details, please."

"I'll get back to you on that."

I figured it had something to do with Shiver's friends at K19 Security Solutions. Perhaps payback, given that Shiver had trained some of their younger team members.

"On that same subject, you'll be meeting Mantis and Alegria at the airfield at zero six hundred. I don't yet know who else they're sending. It's no matter, really. You'll find out in the morning."

"I appreciate this, Shiv," I said.

"You have little recollection of what I owe you, my friend."

I felt my face burning much in the same way Darrow's had at Shiver's thanks. I'd been the first to locate Losha back when she was on the run from United Russia. Their reunion hadn't exactly gone smoothly, but looking across the table at the two of them, made me proud that I'd been a part of it.

When Shiver held up his glass, I did the same.

Esland squeezed my free hand. "I've no idea what he's speaking of, but I'm proud of you nonetheless."

Mrs. Mollybock came in then with the second course. It always made me uncomfortable when she served alone, but the one time I'd gone into the kitchen to offer my help, she'd let me know clearly that she didn't appreciate my suggestion that she was incapable of handling her duties. No amount of explaining that I was simply trying to help, cajoled the woman.

An hour later, I noticed Esland yawn. "Ready to call it a night?"

"I hate to be a spoilsport."

"Let me, then." I looked from her to Darrow and then to Edge. "We have an early departure tomorrow."

"We do," said Darrow, standing at the same time Edge did.

"Thank you for dinner, along with everything else you've done on my behalf," Esland walked over to say to Shiver and Losha, who both hugged her.

"Shall we, then?" I asked, leading her in the direction of the east wing.

"Will this be terribly awkward?" Esland whispered.

"I'm on my way to Covington House to pack, so no, it won't be awkward at all," said Darrow, clearly eavesdropping.

"Don't be an imp," I scolded her.

"You are not the boss of me," she teased. "Oh, wait. Perhaps you are. I hadn't thought of that."

"We'll say our goodbyes tonight," said Shiver. "Godspeed, all. Losha and I will anxiously await our next dinner with you here at the abbey."

The duke and his duchess left in the opposite direction.

"How are you, Ezzie?" I asked as we ascended the staircase.

"Better than I anticipated." She rolled her shoulders. "I suppose it gets easier with time."

I was proud of the way Darrow continued to put her at ease, and I said so.

"It appears we're all growing up."

I wished her voice wasn't tinged with regret, but of course it would be. Gone with our youth were her parents. I had no idea how I'd feel when the day came that I'd have to face the loss of my father.

28

Esland

Axel excused himself to call Z, leaving me in the room where I spent so many nights as a child. The same one in which I'd confessed to Darrow that Axel and I had almost kissed.

Tonight he would share this room with me, and while Darrow said it wouldn't be awkward given she'd be at Covington House, which now belonged to her, I couldn't help but feel uncomfortable.

When Axel came into the room, he joined me at the window seat. Without speaking, he circled my wrist with his fingers and pulled my hand away from my mouth. Before I could disparage myself by mentioning my terrible habit of biting my nails, Axel kissed me.

"I don't like having to share you," he said, unfastening the button of my trousers after pulling my blouse over my head. He led me over to the bed.

"Nor I, you." I reached for him, but he shook his head.

"Let me, Ezzie."

I looked up at him, always taken aback by his handsomeness. Tonight his eyes were the shade of green I loved so much. On their own, they would've melted my heart, but the love I saw gazing back at me almost brought me to tears.

"How did this happen?" I whispered.

"If you mean how did we happen, I've come to believe my father's words. He predicted we would be together long ago. I've learned he's right far more often than wrong. In this case, I couldn't be happier he is."

"You're so bloody sweet I almost can't stand it."

"Let me see what I can do about that."

Axel flipped me to my stomach and pulled me to my knees. I immediately felt his cock inside me. With one hand, he held my breast, his fingers pinching my nipple while he gripped my hip with the other.

"You…are…mine," he said with every thrust into my body. *"Mine."* I felt his lips at the base of my neck and his tongue as it drew a hard line across my shoulders. "Who do you belong to, Ezzie?"

"You, Axel. I'm yours. Now and always." The heady combination of every part of my body being assailed by his sent a jolt of lightning through my frame. When he thrust deeper still, I cried out as a powerful orgasm tore through my body.

"I love you, Esland," he said, shuddering his release. He stilled and I could feel the proof of his climax deep inside me.

He rolled us over so I was on top, straddling him.

"Esland, look at me." It was so hard to keep my eyes open. I was drained of all energy, but I did as he asked. "I'm not sure how to say this, because the last thing I want to apologize for is the absolute best sex I've ever had in my life, but, Ezzie, I didn't use a condom." He held my face in his hands and stared deeply into my eyes.

"I get the shot," I blurted. "I won't get pregnant."

"I want you to know there's never been another time I've done that. Not ever."

I put my fingers on his lips and rested my body on his. "Shh," I said. "It's okay."

He kissed the top of my head. "I love you, Esland. I hope you realize how much."

I felt his lips trailing over my skin again and opened my eyes. "It's time for us to get up, sweetness. I'm sorry it came so quickly. We can, however, sleep on the plane."

"We can?"

Axel nodded and smiled. "I happen to know that there's a stateroom on board."

I sat up. "Seriously?"

"Very seriously."

"My God."

He smiled again. "Right?"

Darrow, who was less of a morning person than me, crawled into the front passenger seat of the 4x4. "I don't suppose any of you considered bringing me coffee," she grumbled.

"Coffee?" I asked.

"Just wait until we get to the ranch and you taste the stuff Quint makes every morning. He'll convert you."

I tensed, wondering what Axel's reaction would be to Darrow speaking of her time in Texas, but he didn't seem to have one at all.

"Close your eyes, sweetness," he murmured. And I did.

When he woke me again, we were on an airfield next to a large plane. Far larger than I'd imagined.

"Is that our plane?"

"It is," Axel answered, holding his hand out to help me from the vehicle.

I didn't see Darrow or Edge and assumed they'd already climbed the stairs that led into the aircraft.

When we did the same, we were greeted by a man and a woman, both in uniform.

"This is Mantis Gehring and his wife, Alegria," said Axel. "May I present Miss Esland Cartwright."

Both held out their hands to shake mine.

"Thank you both for flying over to get us," said Axel, far less formally than the introduction had been.

"Next time give us more notice, and we'll plan a layover in Paris," said Alegria, with a decidedly French accent. "I was born there," she said as an aside.

"One of my favorite cities."

"I don't suppose we have time for a detour." Alegria looked back and forth between Mantis and Axel, but I knew she was joking.

"Next time, my love, I promise," answered her husband. "Make yourselves comfortable." The man motioned them toward the cabin that was set up more like a living room than a traditional aircraft.

Axel led me to two seats that were side by side. I noticed Darrow a few rows away, already looking as though she'd gone to sleep.

"Once we're in the air, feel free to help yourselves to anything in the galley," said Alegria. "It's very well stocked."

"When we reach cruising altitude, you're welcome to either of the staterooms in the back of the plane," Mantis said before taking his wife's hand and returning to the cockpit. "We're scheduled for takeoff in twenty," he said behind him.

"It's so luxurious," I marveled, running my hand over the seat's supple leather.

"Quite," said Axel, raising the armrest between us, fastening my seat belt, and pulling me close to him. "Just wait."

"Have you flown on this plane before?"

Axel nodded. "When Shiver first brought Losha and Kazmir back to London, I traveled with them. Then, like now, a K19 pilot transported us."

"I didn't realize the connection was so close."

"Shiv and Doc, the founding partner of the firm, are as close as brothers. In fact, at one point, Doc asked Shiver to partner with him. Oh, and I don't know if this name means anything to you, but Merrigan Shaw is Doc's wife."

"Merrigan bloody Shaw?"

Axel laughed. "Evidently, you've heard of her."

"Has anyone not? Talk about the female equivalent of James Bond. Has Darrow met her?"

He laughed again. "Of course she has."

"I'm envious."

"When we land, I'll see if she and Doc have a visit to the ranch planned. If not, I'll see what I can do."

"Seriously, Axel? It would be a dream come true to meet her."

He leaned forward and kissed my cheek. "I intend to make all your dreams come true, sweet Ezzie."

We hadn't been in the air long when Alegria opened the cockpit door. "Mantis says you're good to unfasten your seat belts and move about if you'd like." She winked before closing the door again.

"Right or left?" I looked up, startled to see a groggy-looking Darrow staring down at us impatiently.

"Whichever you'd prefer, have at it," Axel responded.

"Good," she grumbled, walking toward the aft of the plane.

"Evidently, she's flown on this plane as well."

Axel didn't answer, and I had no intention of pressing. The less information about their travels as a couple, the better as far as I was concerned.

I followed Axel in the same direction Darrow had gone, and walked in when he opened the cabin door.

"Oh my God," I groaned at the sight of the king-size bed. "If I didn't love you already, I certainly would now."

"Not my plane, sweetness."

"No, but you brought me to it. Good enough." I launched myself on the mattress. "Be a dear and close the door, Axel."

Before it was all the way shut, I had half my clothes off.

"I bet Max would've owned a plane like this if they existed back in his day," I commented, hands behind my head, which rested on the pillow.

"I'm sure you're right," said Axel, dropping his trousers and standing gloriously naked in front of me.

"I could get used to this mode of travel."

"Yeah? Fancy yourself buying a plane, Ezzie?"

"I could do, I suppose. According to Mr. Nicholas, I could right well afford it." I turned to my side when Axel lay next to me. "You know I'm kidding, right?"

"Whether you are or not matters little to me. Whatever you want, you should have. You are more than deserving."

"I'm not worthy of such proclamations, Axel."

"Of course you are, sweetness."

29

Pinch

When I'd stepped out of the bedroom Esland and I shared last night, my original intention was solely to call Z. Instead, Shiver had met me halfway down the staircase.

"I meant to talk to you about Esland's trust," he'd said.

"Right. I completely forgot you mentioned it."

Shiver led me downstairs and into the drawing room, and closed the door.

"Along with the danger Esland is facing due to the investigation into the Football Governing Organization, there may be additional danger relating to her trust."

"By way of?"

"There's rumor of another heir; however, the connection is somewhat distant."

"I take it you don't know who this heir is."

"I do not."

Before going upstairs to where my sweet Ezzie waited, I'd called Z to report the rumor Shiver spoke of, along with my request that Pique be reassigned. I also suggested that George take over as lead on the investigation while I was in the States, and Z agreed.

Thus, there wasn't much for me to do besides wait for my team to sort through the evidence and schedule interviews. I wasn't used to inactivity and felt anxious and out of sorts because of it.

How had Shiver, and even Wilder, let go of the daily grind that came along with the life of an agent?

I looked down at Esland, sound asleep with her head on my chest. She was restless too; I could sense it. She was an investigator as much as I was. I decided then that when she woke, I'd tell her the news Shiver had shared with me about the possibility of another heir. That might be something she and Darrow could sink their teeth into once we arrived in Texas.

When I heard a knock at the door, I startled awake. I eased out from under Esland, pulled on my trousers, and opened it.

"We'll be landing in thirty minutes," Edge told me, peeking around me at Ezzie's sleeping form. "You should probably wake her."

"Thanks." I closed the door and turned around, relieved to see that the bedclothes were covering Esland's nakedness.

"I heard," she said, sitting up. "I can't believe I slept as long as I did."

"You needed the rest."

"What's next?"

"Once we land in Dallas, we'll go straight to the ranch."

"I didn't realize it was a direct flight. I suppose when you're not flying commercial, you can do whatever you like."

"As long as fuel isn't an issue."

She half laughed and looked up at the ceiling. "It's a life unlike I've ever known."

I sat down on the bed. "I had a conversation with Shiver last evening about your trust."

She propped herself up on her elbows.

"He believes there may be another heir, albeit a distant one."

"Does that mean I don't have to worry about becoming an heiress? I have to admit that would be a relief."

I couldn't have predicted Esland's words. How many people, upon hearing they would soon be wealthy beyond their wildest dreams, would then feel relief at the possibility it wasn't true?

"I'm afraid that isn't what he meant. Only that upon your death the other heir would inherit, given you have no heirs of your own."

Her eyes stayed focused on mine as she processed what I was telling her. "Is this heir aware of that possibility? I mean, I knew nothing of the trust at all until yesterday."

"I cannot answer in that Shiver also didn't know who the supposed heir was."

"Our worlds aren't so different."

I cocked my head.

"Leads come in to the *Times*; editors assign reporters to follow up on them. That's if a reporter didn't generate the lead him or herself. A fraction of the time, the story pans out. The balance doesn't go anywhere."

"This lead would be a good one for you to follow."

Her eyes opened wider. "Seriously? You're suggesting I investigate this myself?"

I leaned forward and kissed the tip of her nose. "Sarcasm—"

"Right, right. I get it. At the very minimum, it's a relief to know I don't have to hide doing so."

I laughed. "Who's the imp, you or Darrow?"

"Both, I think. Does this mean you'll be returning my laptop and you might even give me a mobile?"

"You're pressing it, sweetness, but yes. You'll get both."

She mocked me further by clapping her hands with feigned glee.

"Given Darrow's recently granted security clearances, it might be a good thing for the two of you to take on jointly."

"What will you be about?"

"I'm uncertain at this point."

"Meaning?"

I ran the fingers of one hand through my hair that was in desperate need of a trim. "I may have made myself irrelevant."

"Perhaps you can help on the ranch."

Two hours later, we drove into the gates of King-Alexander Ranch. I'd already seen a map with the layout including the details of the security systems in place on the property.

In-ground sensors throughout were used to detect physical movement, acoustic signals, and vibrations, along with a multi-drone surveillance system that made use of thermal sensors capable of approaching areas of interest once a further investigation command was given.

Each of the ranch's buildings, including the main residence, were secured with the latest in surveillance and facial recognition capabilities. Esland, Darrow, Edge, and I, along with the support team coming in from K19, had been front-loaded into the system.

To my knowledge, neither Darrow nor Edge had been briefed on the various systems' operations. That would be first on my agenda once we'd unloaded our gear.

As promised, I'd be returning Esland's laptop and tablet, along with a new mobile. Additionally, she would be armed. Z had questioned that particular decision but ultimately agreed it was my call, as was most everything in regard to this investigation.

I had a conference call scheduled with George tomorrow, and planned to ask Esland to participate along with Darrow, Edge, and maybe Quint, depending on how the man felt about doing so.

"I can see the wheels turning inside your head," Esland whispered. "It's hot."

"It's what?" I whispered in return, grinning.

"You in full MI5 mode. Very hot."

Darrow heard, rolled her eyes, and laughed. "You two are so adorable," she said, repeating her words from the night before. I glared at her, but that only made her laugh harder.

Quint was waiting outside the residence when we drove up. I exited the 4x4 first and held my hand out to Esland, who followed. Darrow and Edge exited from the other side.

"Welcome," Quint said, approaching the group.

He shook my hand, then Edge's, followed by Esland's. When the man approached Darrow, rather than holding out his hand, he put his arms around her and spun her in a circle in the air.

"Welcome back," I heard him say.

Both Edge and I walked to the vehicle and began unloading bags.

"Are you okay?" Esland asked, coming to stand beside me.

"If you mean, am I okay with Quint and Darrow, I promise that I could not care less."

When she raised a brow, I circled her waist with one arm, cupped her cheek with the other hand, and kissed her. "When will you believe that she and I have truly moved on and are far happier now than we were?"

Esland shrugged. "I suppose you have seen the two together previously. It's a first for me."

"I'm happy for her, and if it doesn't work out between them, I'll be happy for her when she meets someone else. Regardless, her state of being single or part of a couple has no bearing whatsoever on how I feel about you."

"Okay."

"Okay? We'll not speak of it again?"

"We'll see."

"I'd hoped Mantis and Alegria would be joining us," Quint said when we sat down for dinner.

"They had to fly straight to California to bring whoever Shiver has arranged as support back here." I looked from Esland to Darrow. "I was telling Ezzie that you've met Merrigan Shaw."

"Right," Darrow said, looking at Esland rather than me. "That woman is my hero. Did you know that Sir Ranald originally asked her to take over as chief of MI6?"

"It wouldn't surprise me," Esland responded. "Her accomplishments are legendary. I told Axel I'm envious you've met her. I hope I get to one day."

"You should reach out," Darrow said to me.

I shrugged and didn't make eye contact. I already had, and by tomorrow, another of Ezzie's dreams would come true.

After we'd landed in Dallas, I'd excused myself and contacted Shiver, who told me he no longer needed to serve as go-between. "Contact Merrigan directly. As managing partner, she'll be able to tell you who they've assigned to Esland's detail."

I hadn't wasted time beating around the bush. I straight off told Merrigan how much Esland admired her. "She hopes one day to meet you," I'd added.

As I'd hoped, the woman immediately offered to fly in the next day along with her husband, Ranger Messick, and Diesel Jacks, the two men she'd given the assignment to assist with Esland's detail.

"You've gone awfully quiet, Fulton," murmured Ezzie.

"Just tired and anxious to be alone with you."

She rested her head on my shoulder. "I know I slept the entire flight, but I'm quite exhausted myself. Would it be terribly rude if we begged off?"

I looked over at Quint and Darrow, who were deep in conversation. Edge looked equally as tired as I felt. I'd planned a briefing tonight, but there was no reason it couldn't wait until tomorrow. That way I could include Ranger and Diesel as well.

"I doubt they'd even notice we left," she added.

"Let's go, then." I stood and motioned for Edge to join us. As Esland had predicted, neither Quint nor Darrow appeared to notice us leave.

30

Esland

"Good morning," I said to Darrow when I found her in the ranch house's kitchen.

"Good morning, True," she responded, walking over to kiss my cheek. "How'd you sleep?"

"I slept fine, but who are you?"

Darrow laughed. "I slept quite well too, thanks. Coffee or tea?"

"Tea, please."

"Have a seat; it'll just be a minute."

"Darrow Whittaker, I've known you most of my life, and you are not a morning person."

"I know," she said, coming to sit next to me. "It's just that when I'm here, I am. I mean, God, Quint and the rest of the ranch hands are up before dawn. If I sleep until eight, I feel like a sloth."

"Wow." I shook my head. "So, are you two, you know, together?"

"For now, we are. When I go back to England, I've no idea what will happen. And after, well, I am training to serve SIS in some form."

"What about training here, like your brother mentioned?"

"We'll see. Somehow I doubt that it's truly a possibility although it would be something." Darrow stood when the tea kettle whistled. "Where is Axel? Still sleeping?"

"No, making calls."

"There was a time that would've raised my ire. I hated being left out, more than I can tell you. Do you feel that way?"

"I suppose it depends on whether Axel stays true to his word and lets me work on the investigation alongside the rest of you."

"Is that a possibility?"

I nodded. "In fact, he has something for us to work on together."

"Who us?"

"You and me."

"You're joking?"

"I'm not."

Darrow rested her elbows on the table. "Well done, my friend. I admit, I didn't think he had it in him."

Without seeing him come in, I felt Axel's presence.

"What happened to not saying a disparaging word about me?" he said to Darrow while coming up behind me and kissing the back of my neck. "Where's Quint this morning?"

"He should be back soon," Darrow answered, looking at the clock. "He typically comes in for breakfast about this time." She stood, walked over to the kitchen, and began pulling food from the refrigerator.

"You're cooking breakfast?" Axel asked.

Darrow raised the pan she had just gotten out of the cupboard. "Watch it," she told him. "Quint thinks I'm an excellent cook."

The two were behaving more and more like brother and sister.

"Good morning," said Edge, joining us at the dining table and looking as though he'd been up for hours. "Quint said he'll be in as soon as he washes up."

"Did you ride out with him?" Darrow asked.

Edge nodded.

"Now I feel like a sloth," I told Axel, repeating Darrow's words.

"See? I told you!"

As Edge said, Quint came in a few minutes later, and we all sat down to breakfast. I offered to help more than once, but both times Darrow shooed me off.

"What's the plan for today?" Darrow asked while everyone else ate the delicious food she'd made.

"The K19 team will arrive shortly after eleven hundred hours."

"Who's coming?" asked Quint.

"I'm not entirely certain," Axel fibbed.

I set my fork down and studied him.

"What?"

"You know very well who's coming. No lying, Fulton."

"All right," he said, laughing at my calling him out. "Ranger and Diesel. Do those names mean anything to you?"

Shrugging, I picked up my fork and continued eating. "This really is fabulous, Darrow. Well done."

"True tells me there's an assignment for us to work together."

"Right," said Axel, finishing the last bite of food on his plate and looking at Quint. "Call is yours, mate. If you prefer I not talk missions around you, I'm happy not to, but on the other hand, you've been around this business all of your life."

"You never offered me the same courtesy," grumbled Darrow.

Quint reached over and rubbed her shoulder. "And if he had, maybe you wouldn't be livin' your dream, darlin'."

I decided Quint's laid-back demeanor was good for my friend. He didn't call her out; he just soothed her.

"I don't mind either way," Quint said to Axel. "Just so you know, I do have third-level clearance."

"I did know, but thanks for confirming. Very well, then, I'll brief you all now and then do it again when the K19 team arrives."

Axel gave everyone at the table the rundown of what I'd found in my mother's diaries. He laid out the doping as well as the sexual abuse conspiracies, and briefed them about what was being done at MI5 headquarters and by whom.

"There's another issue that needs looking into," he said, turning to me as though he was asking if it was okay for him to proceed. I nodded and he did.

"Esland has recently learned of a trust originally put in place by Lord Maxwell Westbrook, her great-grandfather."

"Max is your grandfather?" Darrow gasped.

"He is," I answered, nodding.

"Why didn't you ever say?"

I shrugged. "It never came up."

Axel let out a sigh. "Anyway, this trust is significant."

"It would be," commented Darrow, which garnered another glare from Axel. "Sorry, go ahead."

"Later we'll speak about appropriate behavior during briefings," he muttered in her direction. "As I was saying, Shiver received intel suggesting there may be another heir. He has no further information, other than this heir would only inherit upon Esland's passing."

Darrow took a breath as though she was about to speak, but sat back in her chair instead.

"Given that, he does believe there may be a threat potential. Also, given that Esland's mother was an only child as was her grandmother, the heir would have to be descended from a sibling or even cousin of Lord Westbrook himself."

"We can get started immediately," I said. "By way of genealogy."

"Precisely," he said before looking at Quint. "My understanding is there are two networks."

Getting up from the table, Quint walked into the kitchen. "It's coded. Once you enter it, you'll need a unique password that will be issued by SIS."

"Thank you," I said when the man handed me a card.

"Darrow, you'll need your own, as will everyone else. Access will be given via your thumbprint, which I'm told was preloaded."

"That's right," said Axel, looking from Quint to Edge, then Darrow, and finally at me. "We've cut no corners in regard to your safety," he said solemnly. "There are access points all over the ranch that allow entry only via either facial or other biorecognition."

Darrow was smiling and I understood why. This was the stuff of my friend's dreams as a child, to be on the inside of intelligence rather than a presumed-ignorant bystander.

"Any questions?" Axel asked. When no one responded, he motioned for me to follow.

Once back in the room we'd share the night before, he pulled out a case. "This, you will recognize as your laptop, however, with the addition of the security features we've just discussed. The setup is the same on your tablet and new mobile."

"Thank you, Axel."

His expression switched from professionally stern to indulgent. "You're welcome, Ezzie. I have something else to tell you. I was going to keep it a surprise, but I find I selfishly want to keep your smile all to myself when you find out."

I raised a brow.

"You were right to say that I was fibbing earlier. I do know who is coming in from K19."

"Merrigan?"

Axel nodded, and I threw my arms around his neck.

"Thank you," I repeated again and again as I kissed him. "I can't believe I'm actually going to meet her."

"She's as human as the rest of us, Ezzie."

"No, she bloody isn't. God, does Darrow know?"

"Certainly not. I wouldn't risk her spoiling my surprise."

I checked the time. "She'll be here in a few hours?"

"That's right."

"Excuse me, Axel, but I need to prepare."

He kissed my forehead, but I wasn't going to let him go that easily. "Wait," I said, pulling him into my arms and crushing my mouth to his. When he put his hands on my arse, I lifted my legs and wrapped them around his waist.

"You need to prepare," he muttered before diving back in for another kiss.

"Not until I thank you properly."

31

Pinch

After leaving Ezzie a well-sated woman, I walked outside to return George's call. I'd expected to hear from her this morning, provided Z briefed her on her taking the lead in the UK, and neither disappointed.

"Pinch," she said, answering my call. "Thank you for getting back to me so quickly."

"Can we drop the pretense, George? You and I have never been adversaries, and we aren't now."

I heard her take a deep breath. "You're right, Pinch. My apologies."

"What's happening over there, George? You and Z have seemed at odds the last few times I've seen you."

"I'm not sure how to respond. Z is as professional with me as anyone else."

Interesting in that I didn't say anything about professionalism in the same way I hadn't mentioned gender bias to Edge.

"Very well," I responded. "Give me an update on Pique's status."

"Bugger me," George groaned. "That was properly bodged."

"How so?"

"Z had me communicate his reassignment right after you rang him. Pique went right off his trolley over it."

"What did he do?"

"Took holiday with no notice."

"Where is he?"

"No one knows."

"Bugger me." I'd ask if she was serious if I wasn't already certain she was. How could the United Kingdom's domestic counterintelligence and security agency not know where one of our own agents was? This was so far beyond bad form.

I already had a terrible feeling about Pique, only made worse by this news. Later, I'd follow up with Z about it. Maybe Pique informed him of his travel plans directly. Even thinking it, sounded ludicrous. If Z knew where the man was, so would George.

"What was his next assignment?"

"That's just it, al-Qaeda cells. What want would he have to investigate footballers over domestic terrorism?"

I murmured my agreement. "Shall we get on with the footballers, then? Before I forget, you mentioned that when Graham and Veronica Cartwright died, you didn't think it was an accident either. Why not?"

"As it happened, my family lived fairly close to the accident site. There was evidence of not just one other car, but two. I followed the press coverage closely and was aghast that it wasn't ever investigated as such."

"Did you act on it?"

"I did, and I was immediately shut down."

"By whom?"

"Nate Thomason."

"Bugger me," I muttered again.

Nate had been Wilder's second-in-command, and Sir Ranald Caird's before that. I'd been part of the team investigating him, which had culminated in the man being taken into custody a few short weeks ago. He was currently awaiting trial, which meant that MI5 had the upper hand in terms of this particular investigation.

"Before you ask, I'm scheduled to question him tomorrow afternoon."

"Outstanding, George. This could be a real break if he knew something then that he'll give up now."

"Right." She sighed again. "Anything else on this?"

"You're in charge, George."

"About that, Axel…"

I waited, but she didn't say anything else. Finally, I did. "I'm confiding in you now, Leighton."

"Understood."

"I have made the suggestion that you'd be the better candidate."

"I find that difficult to believe, Axel."

"Not that this is the sole reason, but I've decided to take my name out of it."

"Why?" she gasped.

"I can't say I'm ready to discuss it. Suffice to say that I'm reevaluating."

"*Bugger me.* You're resigning, aren't you?"

"Don't jump to the same conclusion Z did. All I'm saying is that I've decided against the DG position."

"Very well, Pinch. We'll speak more about this when you return to London. When will that be?"

"I'm not certain, but I assure you I'll be in touch."

"Right," she said before ending the call.

I'd always gotten on well with George, and our estrangement over the job of director general hadn't sat well with me. We were colleagues who had worked as a team for many years. It felt good to be back on that footing with her.

An hour later, I received an alert from the drone system that an approaching vehicle was within a mile of the ranch gate. I zoomed in, fascinated by the technology. I could clearly see Doc and Merrigan in the front, Ranger and Diesel in the back seat.

"They're approaching." I walked in to where Esland sat studying her computer. She scurried toward me, launching herself into my arms.

"I'm beside myself," she said, kissing my face repeatedly.

"I'll have to figure out more ways to get you there. I could get used to the way you show appreciation."

"Just wait until later…Pinch."

She winked when she said it, and I laughed. "You like that, eh?"

Esland shook her head. "I love it." Her expression grew more serious. "I love you, Axel."

"And I, you, Ezzie." My mobile pinged again, and I showed her the screen before leading her outside to wait with me on the porch.

"Where is Darrow?" she asked when the 4x4 was approaching.

"Perhaps she's giving you a moment."

"I knew your mother," Merrigan told Esland when I introduced them and then watched as they walked away arm in arm.

"I'm not sure who was more excited," commented Doc. "Evidently, Merrigan knew Veronica Cartwright quite well."

I led Doc along with the other two K19 operatives inside and briefed them as I had the rest of the group earlier.

"We'll stay on tonight," Doc said, "but we need to leave in the morning due to a prior commitment I regret we couldn't change."

"I appreciate your coming at all. Sincerely."

"I have another item to see to while I'm here. I understand Darrow has joined SIS."

"Training at this point, but yes."

"If you can locate her now and she isn't in the middle of anything else, we can get the next step taken care of."

I was mildly curious, but not enough to ask. This was Darrow's deal, and I was proud of her for it. She'd changed so much in the last few months, there were times I wondered if she was the same woman I'd known most of my life.

"I can alert her," Edge offered.

"Show the men around the ranch while you're at it," I told him.

When the three agents were gone, Doc pushed his chair back and rested his elbows on his knees. "Nasty business," he murmured.

"Right," I agreed. "I'd like to see all those involved executed at dawn by firing squad."

"Those were the good ol' days," said Doc, smiling briefly. "Whatever we can do to help, besides protection, the K19 team is available. On or off the record. This is the kind of thing we'll work for pro bono."

I'd heard rumors about the men and women of K19 throughout the years. The stories sometimes sounded like they'd come straight out of superhero graphic novels.

"While I owe Shiver my life, Merrigan's too, the idea that there were coaches and even players sexually abusing children is more than I can stomach. The rest of the team concurs. We've got a couple of broken wings, but otherwise, everyone is on board if needed."

"Again, I appreciate the offer, Doc. As soon as I know more, you will hear from me."

The man nodded and then stood. When I saw Darrow approaching, I stood too. "I'll leave you, then," I said, shaking Doc's hand.

Once again I found myself without much to do. I went outside and over to the barn where I saw Edge talking to Ranger and Diesel.

"I was filling them in on Pique," Edge said.

"Worked with him a couple of times over in Syria. Diesel and I both did," said Ranger.

"There was something he said once that you might want to look into," added the other man.

"Right," said Ranger. "He was spouting off about being descended from some sort of aristocracy."

I raised a brow.

"Could've been a load of crap, but it would be worth us taking a look."

"He might also have a connection to Willingham Allied, one of the other teams, or even the organization itself," Ranger added.

"Or he's just a bloody wanker." The two laughed at Edge's assessment.

"Could very well be."

"We can start looking, unless there's something else in particular you want us to be doing right now."

"Have at it, gents," I said. "In fact, I'll join you."

I hadn't considered there'd be another reason entirely to explain Pique's behavior, but if either of Ranger and Diesel's theories proved correct, I'd hunt the *sonovabitch* down myself and kill him with my bare hands.

32

Esland

"How did you and my mother meet?" I asked Merrigan.

"She used to child-mind me actually."

"You're kidding!"

Merrigan told me about growing up in the same Notting Hill neighborhood as my mother did and the time they spent together. "She was always so beautiful, even as a teenager," Merrigan said. "And I wasn't."

"I have a hard time believing that."

"Thank you, but it's true. I'll see if I can dig up any photos of us from then. She really was so kind to me. My family had moved from the Isle of Arran shortly before I met Veronica. I can't imagine what lonely hell I would've been in if it weren't for her."

"Did you know my father as well?"

Merrigan put her hand on mine and launched into a string of stories about the time she spent with the two of them together.

Two hours later, I hadn't asked Merrigan a single question that I'd planned to. Instead of a *Times* reporter, I was a girl learning about my parents' lives before I was born. It was a gift I wouldn't have known to ask for, yet it was as precious as any I could imagine.

"Would you fancy some tea?" I asked, feeling parched myself.

"I would, thanks."

We stood to go inside, and Merrigan put her hand on my shoulder. "I loved having this time with you. My memories of Veronica are among my fondest. Thank you."

My eyes filled with tears when the woman I'd always admired from afar hugged me. "I can't thank you enough," I said in return.

"How is our Darrow?" Merrigan asked when we walked inside.

"How well do you know her?"

"Hmm. How to answer? Shiv is like a brother to me, so fairly well."

"Axel said they call her Duchess of Monckton."

Merrigan laughed. "That, I can see."

"All kidding aside, she's doing far better than was expected."

"Not a surprise, really. Good for her that she put her foot down finally."

"Did you know she wanted to work for SIS since she was a young girl?"

"I did."

I set the tea kettle down. I was the first, other than her, to say I knew. "I don't know where she's gone off to, but I'm sure she'd love a visit."

"Kade, or Doc as he was introduced, is insisting we must return to California tomorrow, but given I control our schedules, I'm thinking another day might be in order."

"I would love that, truly."

"Our wee ones are with Kade's parents, Laird and Sorcha—and if you ever find yourself in need of a story, I highly encourage you to write theirs."

Over tea, Merrigan told me about how Doc's parents had met. Sorcha sounded like a hoot, and I hoped I would, one day, have the chance to meet her.

When Darrow appeared, I excused myself to give them time alone to chat. I had no idea where Axel was, either, so I powered up my laptop and started looking into Lord Westbrook's family.

When my eyes began drifting closed, I rested my head on the bed's pillow. The last week had been filled with as much unimaginable horror as unmitigated joy. Apart from my new, and totally unexpected, relationship with Axel, I'd learn so much about my parents. Of course it made me miss them all the more, but the stories, especially those about my mother, made me feel closer somehow.

"I'll do this, Mum," I said to the empty room. "I'll finish what you began, and I'll see justice for your death. Pops' too."

I let my eyes drift closed then, hoping that in my dreams, my parents would pay me a visit.

When I woke, Axel's arm was around my waist and he was asleep too. What comfort that gave me. I wiggled my bottom in the hope it would wake him, only to find he hadn't really been asleep.

"How long have you been stretched out behind me?" I asked.

"Only a few minutes, although I'd happily stay here the rest of the day."

"Me too."

"How was your time with Merrigan?"

I launched into a recounting of most of our conversation, thinking every so often that Axel would be bored, but whenever I paused, he asked more about it.

"You're very sweet," I said, looking over my shoulder.

"You remember what happened the last time you said that to me."

"I do, which is why I said it again."

Rolling off the bed, Axel walked over to the door and locked it. Then he picked up my mobile and turned it off, followed by his.

"I've told you before I don't like sharing you," he growled as he grabbed my feet and pulled me to the end of the bed.

Expecting him to undress me, I was surprised when he removed his clothes first.

"I like this," I said when he stood before me naked.

"Just wait. You'll like what I do next so much more."

I giggled when he tore at my clothes, tickling me as much as removing them.

"I love the sound of your laughter," he said, holding me still and looking into my eyes. "I want to spend the rest of my life making you giggle, admiring you as you spend endless days unabashedly naked in our home. I want to make sweet babies with you that I pray, for their sake, look far more like you than me. I want this to be our life, Ezzie. You and me. I don't care if I see the inside of another office or case file. I don't want to accept another mission that might take me away from you a day let alone weeks at a time."

When he eased his grip on me, I rested my head on his heart. "What's wrong, Axel?"

"There's not a thing wrong, except for the way my life was before you came into it."

I ran my fingers through his hair. As much as I loved his passion, I loved this too.

"There are times I find myself wondering if this could possibly be real."

"It doesn't seem possible to me sometimes either, but I know what I feel, Ezzie."

When we heard a knock at the bedroom door, Axel pulled the bedclothes over me and put on his trousers. "Coming," he said when we heard the knock again.

When I saw Darrow on the other side of the threshold, in tears, I sat up.

"It's Wellie," she said, dissolving into sobs in Axel's arms.

I turned my head away, feeling as though I was intruding on a moment too private, too intimate. My heart broke for them both as Axel and Darrow cried in one another's arms. This was not the time to feel jealousy, but I did, and it made me feel equally disgusted with myself. The man I loved had lost his father. If it was Darrow who could give him the most comfort, then I should step aside and allow him that.

I eased from the bed, grabbed my clothes as quietly as I could, and slipped out the patio door. I hurriedly threw my jumper over my head, pulled on my trousers, and slid my feet into my shoes. I hadn't bothered to grab my knickers or bra in my haste.

Instead of going around the front of the ranch house, I walked farther around the back to where I'd seen some outbuildings. There was a light on in one. Maybe there I'd find Quint or one of the other hands who could reach him and let him know what had happened in the event Darrow needed him.

The hinge creaked when I opened the door. "Hello," I said to the man whose back was to me. "I'm wondering if you know where Quint might be?"

I walked closer, thinking perhaps the man hadn't heard me. "Excuse me?" I said, again trying to get his attention.

"No hablo ingles," he said when he turned to me.

"Oh, dear, and I don't speak Spanish," I muttered. "Quint? Uh…" I wasn't sure what else to say. How could a man work here and not know the name? At that moment, the door creaked again and he looked beyond me. When I turned around, my heart stopped.

"What are you doing here, Pique?" I asked as he crept closer.

"I think you know."

When I felt the other man approaching from behind, I tried to get around Pique, but he grabbed me at the same time I felt something hit the back of my head.

"I told you not to kill her yet!" I heard someone shout before I lost consciousness. It didn't sound like Pique's voice, but it was familiar.

33

Pinch

"Where is Esland?" I asked, turning around to look for her as I wiped my tears.

"I don't know. She was just here," answered Darrow.

I walked over to the bedside table and picked up the mobile I'd turned off. I waited while it powered up, stunned when it did and no messages or texts were waiting.

"Who contacted you?" I asked Darrow while I waited for Shiver to answer.

"Thornton sent a text saying he was gone and to tell you…" Darrow dissolved back into tears. "I tried to ring him, but the call didn't go through, so I came to find you. I'm so sorry, Axel."

I looked at the screen on my mobile. "My call isn't going through either. Let me see his message."

She handed it to me.

"Swipe it and then enter your code."

When she tried, first nothing happened, and then an error message came on the screen.

"Try again."

She did and got the same error message.

"Something's off. We need to find Esland." There were only two ways out of the bedroom, and we'd been standing in one; she had to have gone out the back.

Darrow nodded but seemed too stunned to move.

"Darrow!" I shouted, shaking her. "You go find Doc or Quint, anyone at all. I'll go around back and look for Esland."

When I pushed her, it seemed to jar her out of her fog, and she ran toward the kitchen. I raced out of the patio slider.

The first thing I needed to do was find Esland. Once I had, I'd figure out how to reach Shiver and get the details about my father.

Remembering the drone coverage, I tried to pull the system controls up on my mobile, but the same error message Darrow had gotten appeared on my screen.

"Bugger me," I spat as a feeling of dread settled over me. Something was terribly wrong, and I had a horrible feeling it wasn't with my father.

When I saw no sign of Esland, I kept going around the house. When I reached the front, Doc, Merrigan, and Darrow were there, waiting.

"I haven't been able to find Quint."

"I haven't seen Esland either."

Both Doc and Merrigan were fussing with their mobiles. "Something has jammed the signal," said Doc, pulling out his gun. He fired once, counted five seconds, and then fired again, repeating the sequence one more time.

We waited a few moments but didn't see anyone or hear a response.

"I know the property. I can head out on horseback," said Darrow.

"I'll go with you." Merrigan pointed to their vehicle. "Kade, you and Axel take the 4x4 and look as well."

Doc was already inside the SUV by the time Merrigan finished her sentence. He tried to start it, but it wouldn't turn over.

"There are ATVs in the barn!" Darrow shouted, running toward it. Doc and I followed.

Where in bloody hell was everyone? Quint, Edge, Ranger, and Diesel, along with the other men that worked this ranch seemed to have disappeared.

"Jesus bloody Christ!" I shouted when I saw boots sticking out of one of the stalls.

Merrigan raced over in front of me. *"It's Edge!"* she shouted. "He has a pulse. I'll stay with him; you go!"

Darrow had the keys to the ATVs. "This will be faster than on horseback," she said, tossing one set to me.

"I'm going to see if I can sort out the security system," said Doc.

"Do you know where it's housed?"

"No, but I know where to start looking."

"I'll head north," I said, trying to remember as much as I could about the ranch's layout given my mobile appeared dead.

Darrow gave me a thumbs-up.

We were quickly losing daylight, and while the ATVs had lights, the darker it got, the harder it would be to find anyone out on the ranch land.

As I drove the vehicle out of the barn, I noticed the outbuildings toward the back of the house. Why in bloody hell hadn't I checked those before?

I raced over and climbed off the ATV with the lights shining on the pathway to the door. I could hardly see, but it appeared there were fresh footprints. I pulled out my mobile, hoping at least the flashlight app would work well enough to illuminate the interior of the building.

I skirted past the prints as to not disturb them, pulled my sleeve down over my hand, and opened the door. I could see what looked like a man's body facedown on the dirt floor, raced over, and felt for a pulse. When I couldn't find one, I flipped the body over. It was no one I recognized, but he hadn't been dead long.

I shone the light around the building but didn't see anyone else. I raced over to the next one. Since there were no visible footprints going into the dilapidated structure, I went around the outside of it, doing my best not to disturb any tracks there might be.

I heard three shots fired at five-second intervals in the distance and raced to the ATV.

Whatever, whoever, it was, it was a distress signal, and I had to respond to it. I fired once in response and waited until I heard two more shots, again at five-second intervals. I went in the direction of the gunfire as fast as the ATV would take me, praying the ground I was traversing was flat and even enough for me to navigate.

I came to a crest and didn't see any sign of Darrow or light from the ATV, so I fired again and waited for a response. Seconds later, I heard two more shots that sounded as though they were coming from the south.

Even the light of the moon was obscured by thick cloud cover as I raced over the rough terrain with nothing but instinct guiding me.

I came upon another crest and saw light not too far off in the distance.

As I approached, I could see one man sitting on the ground and what appeared like two more dead bodies.

"We were ambushed," shouted Quint when I was close enough to hear him. "Your men are alive. It wasn't their intent to kill us, just to slow us down."

"Were you on horseback?" I asked, climbing off the ATV and racing over to where Darrow tended to Ranger and Diesel.

"Like I said, we were ambushed. Must've been ten of them at least. Might've had a chance, but we weren't on the horses at the time. Bastards must've scared 'em off after they knocked us out."

"Did you see or hear anything?"

"They were Englishmen; I can tell you that much."

My eyes met Darrow's.

"I don't know what to pray for, Axel," she said.

"Pray it was a trick."

She nodded and helped Ranger sit up when he came to. Quint got to his feet and got on the back of the ATV just as Diesel came to as well.

"What the fuck?" he groaned, trying to sit up. I caught him as he fell back toward the ground.

"It'll be easier for me to find my way back to you. I'll take Ranger and come back with the truck."

"They've been disabled," Darrow told him.

"The Bummer sure as hell hasn't," Quint shouted as he raced off on the ATV.

I looked at Darrow while I waited for Diesel to get his bearings. "What's he talking about?"

"It's...I don't know how to explain it, but he's probably right. No one would know how to disable it, let alone find it."

Diesel groaned and rubbed his head. When he held out his hand, it was bloody. "Help is on the way," Darrow told him and then turned to me. "Go. I'll wait here for Quint to come back."

I didn't wait for her to change her mind. I had no idea where I was going or what I was looking for. All I knew was I couldn't sit doing nothing while Esland was out there somewhere in what I sensed was grave danger.

I was several hundred yards away when I felt my mobile vibrate. I stopped and pulled it out.

"Pinch," I answered.

"It's Merrigan. Kade has been able to get the security systems back online as well as disable the signal blockers. Both local law enforcement and emergency responders are on their way."

"Tell them to come in silent and dark."

"Right," answered Merrigan.

If there was anything to report on Esland, that would've been the first thing she told me, so I didn't bother to ask. "I'm on my way back now."

"Good. Kade is reprogramming the drones now."

As I drove, I silently prayed both for Esland's safety and that the reports of my father's death were a trick in order to distract us. Both were too much to hope for; I knew that. I also knew that if I could only pray for one, my father would tell me to pray for Esland.

I could see the barn and the lights from the emergency vehicles from where I stopped. I pulled my mobile back out of my pocket, looked up at the sky, dialed my father's cottage, and waited while it rang.

34

Esland

"How could you have been so fucking stupid?" I heard a voice shout. I was blindfolded, but still prayed no one was watching close enough to tell I'd come to.

"It was the only way we could know whether the diaries contained any evidence." Both voices sounded familiar, but with the throbbing in my head, I couldn't focus enough to identify them.

I heard what sounded like a fist come down on a table and steeled myself from reacting.

"You were supposed to destroy them!"

"The room is monitored around the clock. I told you again and again there would be no way for me to do so."

"Kill him," I heard the one voice say, followed by a single gunshot, and then...sobbing. Evidently, they hadn't actually shot the man I now knew was Hodges.

"Where are they now?" someone demanded.

More sobbing.

"Fucking answer me!"

"M…I…5."

My fingernails dug into the palms of my hands as I waited for what would come next. Maybe with all that was going on, no one was paying attention to me.

Another shot rang out, and this time, I somehow knew Hodges was dead. There was no point in keeping him alive since MI5 had my mother's diaries. He'd failed, and they'd killed him for it. But what did they want with me? I couldn't procure the diaries for them either, and if they somehow thought I could, MI5 already had all the evidence they needed.

"What do you want to do with her?" I heard another voice ask.

"I haven't bloody decided yet."

Suddenly someone grasped my hair, pulling my head up. "She's come to."

"Take care of it," the voice that seemed so bloody familiar shouted.

I felt a cloth cover my mouth, and everything went black.

35

Pinch

It was after midnight in Bedfordshire, but I still prayed against hope that by some miracle my father would answer his telephone. He couldn't really be dead, could he? Wouldn't I feel differently somehow if he were?

I counted the rings…eight…nine…ten.

"Hello, Axel?" my father's groggy voice answered. "What's wrong, son?"

My eyes filled with tears of relief. I almost sobbed. "Someone has Esland, Pops."

"Dear God in heaven," my father gasped. "I'm sorry, Axel. I'll say every prayer."

"Thanks, Pops."

"What else?"

"Nothing, Pops. Just pray I find her."

I couldn't bring myself to tell him that someone had tricked Darrow into thinking he was dead. Or that I'd been praying for both him and Esland, knowing that only one might get answered. And it had.

I turned the key in the ATV and closed the distance between where I'd stopped and the barn.

"Ranger and Diesel are going to be okay, as is Edge," said Darrow, who Quint had obviously been able to fetch.

"Right," I murmured, knowing too much time had passed for us to find Esland. Whoever took her could be anywhere by now. And we had no leads since the fucking state-of-the-art security system had been so easily sabotaged. The list of people who would face my wrath was growing exponentially longer by the minute.

"I think I might've hit on something," said Doc, motioning me over to where he stood near the barn studying something that looked like an oversized tablet.

When I stood next to him, he pointed to an area that looked much like the first outbuildings I'd checked.

"Whoever hacked into the system must not have realized that the drones would continue recording even when sabotaged. They didn't shut them down completely, although they probably thought they had," he explained. "Essentially, all they did was block the signals temporarily."

I nodded, watching what the drones had recorded. The heat and vibration sensors had kicked in, but with no one to manually tell the software to zoom in, there was no detail. In this case, we didn't need it.

"Where is this?" I shouted to Quint as I watched the screen.

"About three miles due south." He pointed to the largest structure. "That's a cowshed; it's all open. The smaller structures are where we keep equipment. Those are enclosed buildings. Looks like they're in the shop area."

Quint pointed in the opposite direction, to what looked like a vehicle that had been spray-painted with a yellow texture. "We'll take the Bummer."

I hadn't closed the door of the…whatever the fuck it was, before Quint had it screaming down the dirt road.

There were four rows of seats, including the front bench seat, none of which looked like they were even bolted down. Doc, Edge, Diesel, and Ranger held onto whatever they could find. When the vehicle hit one crest, all four men in the back hit the roof as the Bummer went momentarily airborne.

Quint slammed on the brakes, turned off the lights, shut off the engine, and motioned in the direction each of us should go in. I took off running; Darrow was right behind me. As we got closer to the building, I slowed, creeping through the brush. I turned around and could see Darrow, but if I hadn't, I wouldn't have known she was there. As it was, she was my shadow.

I motioned with my head for her to go to the left window of the building while I went to the right on the same side. What I'd thought were windows, were actually more like places where someone left an opening between cinder blocks.

From where I stood, I could see the left side of the building where three men stood. It was too dark to be able to identify them, but when one spoke, I recognized his voice immediately as belonging to the bloody bastard Charlie Ambrose. If I had to guess, Pattison was in there too.

While I couldn't see the right side of the building at all from where I stood, I could hear voices coming from that direction. When I heard another man's voice, I wanted to crash through the cinder blocks and kill him with my bare hands.

"She's no use alive," I heard Pique say. "MI5 has the evidence. Even if you were able to retrieve it, it's too late. Most of it has been scanned into evidence already. I need the bitch *dead.* Once she is, you'll have more money than you know what to do with to silence what few witnesses are left—by any means possible."

"What the fuck are you about?" the man I guessed was Pattison shouted. "You don't fucking tell us what to do. You wanna end up like this wanker? Keep running your bloody mouth, and I'll see to it you do. You didn't deliver any better than he did. 'I'm on the bloody case. I'll intercept the diaries.' Fucking useless is what you are."

"Don't forget there's close to a billion pounds on the line, which you won't get any of if you kill me."

I caught Darrow's head movement from the corner of my eye. I crept down and made my way over to her.

"What was that?" one of the men said, looking toward the other side of the structure.

"Settle the fuck down, Beau. Probably an animal," said Pique. "I told you the security systems as well as mobile signals have been scrambled. They'll never bloody find us."

"I pulled the starters on all of the vehicles," said another voice.

I nodded. Beau Pattison. I'd thought so. That meant, inside, there were two former footballers, Pattison and Ambrose, one *former* MI5 agent, and at least two other people besides Esland, one of whom was dead.

"Make a bloody decision whether you want to kill her or keep her alive. We need to get the fuck out of here," grunted Ambrose, the pitch level and hoarseness of his voice betraying his years of steroid use.

Darrow flinched, just barely, but I felt it. "He's got her," she mouthed, raising her gun and taking aim. There wasn't enough room in the space between the cinder blocks for me to do the same, nor could I tell Darrow to move out of my way. If she believed she had the shot, I couldn't give her any reason whatsoever to doubt herself. Esland's life depended on Darrow trusting her training as well as herself, and acting on both.

"When you've got the shot, bloody take it," I whispered. She nodded once, adjusting her aim while I crept around the other side of the building, prepared to bust through the door as soon as I heard her gun go off. I only prayed that the other guys were preparing to do the same.

As I turned, I saw Quint and Doc positioned by the door I'd been headed for. I pointed out in the air, where the other men were located just inside the door. Doc and Quint nodded.

Within seconds I heard the distinct airy whistle of the suppressor attached to Darrow's firearm. At the same moment we heard the first shot fired, the other men and I burst through the door, each taking down the closest threat.

I looked up and watched the only other person in the building fall to the ground. Darrow's second shot was a direct hit.

I raced over to Esland, bound, gagged, blindfolded, but thank God, breathing. I untied the gag, pulled the blindfold away from her eyes, and tore at the ropes binding her. At the same time, the others checked each of the downed men to make sure they were dead. I almost hoped they all weren't, just so I could shoot them again.

I carried my sweet Ezzie in my arms to where Quint had pulled up in his yellow monstrosity.

"How does she seem?" asked Darrow.

"I don't know yet."

"I was so bloody scared, Axel. Why did my first kill have to be in order to save the life of my best friend?"

When she stepped forward to open the door, Quint took Esland from my arms so I could climb in. Once I had, Quint gently rested her on my lap.

"I'm proud of you, my sweet shadow," I heard the man say to Darrow, and then watched as she fell into his arms, sobbing with what was likely an adrenaline crash.

I remembered thinking the same thing about Darrow earlier. Among SIS agents, her oldest brother, Shiver, was known to be able to get in and out of any situation without anyone seeing or hearing him. Perhaps Darrow possessed some of that same ability.

Doc climbed in next to me and did what he could to check Esland's vitals. "They knocked her out with something; that's obvious, I know." He pulled out his phone and punched at the screen.

"Merrigan says the EMTs are still at the house. They'll be able to do a more thorough job than I can now."

"Thanks, Doc," I muttered as Esland moved slightly in my arms. When I looked down at her beautiful face, she opened her eyes.

"Axel?" she said, bringing one hand to her head. "Where am I?"

"Shh," I murmured, helping her sit up. "You're safe, my love. It's all over."

She closed her eyes again. "What happened? My head is bloody throbbing."

"Don't try to talk yet. We'll be back to the house very soon, and there are emergency personnel waiting to look you over."

"Hodges," she murmured, and I nodded.

"It appears he was in on it."

"And Pique. I knew better than to trust that bloody bastard."

I smiled at Esland's inability to remain quiet even in her groggy state, even to her own benefit.

"What happened to him? I hope you put him in the bloody gallows and whip him daily. Hourly would be better."

"He's dead, sweetness."

"I suppose that's better."

I eased her off of my lap and onto the seat, only because the ride might be less jarring.

Darrow turned around from the front seat, and from where I sat, I could see her eyes meet Esland's, and they were full of tears. "I killed him," she said, barely above a whisper.

"Thank you," Esland whispered in response, tearing up as well. She rested her head on my shoulder. "I'm so sorry about your father," she said, also in a whisper.

"Was a ruse to distract us," I said quietly to her.

"What? He's alive?"

"Talked to him an hour ago, maybe it was longer. To be honest, I've lost all track of time. Anyway, he was fine. Praying for your safety."

"Thank God," she mumbled, looking out into the dark. "What a horrid, horrid thing to do. To make someone think they lost their parent."

I squeezed her hand. "Thank God you're both okay."

When Quint pulled up alongside the ambulances, everyone waited while I got Esland out first. The emergency personnel were waiting with a gurney, which she initially scoffed at until I leveled a stern gaze on her.

"You don't know what you were given, Ezzie. Let them get you checked out."

She sat where they told her to. Soon she was on her back, and they were wheeling her into the house.

"What happened?" I heard Merrigan ask Doc.

"I'm not sure of all the players. We'll wait and let Axel tell you," I also overheard. Yes, there would be reports to file, bodies to collect, investigations to be done, but at that moment, I didn't care about any of it. All I wanted to know was that Esland was going to be okay. I didn't say a word in acknowledgment of having heard Doc's conversation with Merrigan. Instead, I followed Esland inside.

I tried my best to stay out of the way while they looked her over, but when she held her hand out, I was powerless not to take it. I kissed the back of it and then turned it over and kissed her palm. "I love you, Esland," I said, bringing her hand up to my cheek. "I love you so much."

36

Esland

I could hear the EMTs telling Axel that I would be fine. They said to keep an eye on me just in case I had an adverse reaction to being knocked out. I also heard Axel say that if Doc and Merrigan weren't staying at the ranch overnight, he would've insisted I go to the hospital. I would've refused, of course, but that was beside the point.

"Let me carry you into the bedroom," Axel said when the EMT indicated they were finished with their examination.

"Seriously, I'm fine," I scoffed, but it was too late. He'd already scooped me into his arms and made it clear he had no intention of setting me on my feet.

"Just grant me this one concession, Ezzie," he whispered into my ear after kissing my neck just below it.

I rested my head on his shoulder. "Don't we need to talk about what happened tonight?"

"Tomorrow morning will be soon enough."

"What about...I'm not sure how to say this, but... what about Pique's body? You said Darrow killed him."

"The others are dead too, Esland. But it isn't something you need to be concerned with. They're being taken care of. The necessary reports are being prepared as we speak. I'll look at them in the morning as well as take your statement."

Axel set me on the bed and then pulled the bedclothes back.

"I'm so glad Wellie is okay."

"Me too." Axel moved my hands when I began to undress. "Let me."

He slowly removed my clothing, kissing my bare skin as he went. "Under the covers," he said once I was naked.

I grabbed his wrist. "You aren't leaving me alone, are you?"

Axel leaned down and kissed me. "Never again if I can help it."

I smiled. "Thank you, but I think I'll eventually be okay on my own."

Once he was as naked as I was, Axel walked around to the other side of the bed and crawled in next to me. "That doesn't mean I will be. I don't think I've ever been so frightened in my life."

"I'm sure you were more so when Matthew Caird held Darrow, Orina, and baby Kazmir hostage."

"I was, you're right, but not more so. I love you, Esland."

Axel put his arm around me and snuggled me so my head was above his heart. Its beat was strong and consistent, just like he'd been since I walked back inside the pub and asked him to help me.

The minute he'd looked into my eyes, I knew he wouldn't turn me away. I put my arm around his waist and squeezed.

Axel chuckled. "What was that for?"

"Helping me. Rescuing me. Loving me. I love you so much. I hope you know that."

He nodded. "I do, but if you intend to follow that statement with a *but*, I'm telling you that you are stuck with me, Ezzie Cartwright. I'll follow you to the ends of the earth just so I can do this whenever I want to." He put his hand on my chin, leaned down, and kissed me.

"I was scared too."

"I'm sure you were," he said, pulling me even closer. "Do you want to talk about it?"

"I don't know. Part of me thinks it'll help, and the other part thinks it'll just make it worse."

"It's over, Ezzie," he said, kissing the top of my head.

"Is it? You don't think there are others involved?"

"I believe that two of the original ringleaders are dead. While Pique's death will be kept out of the media, Pattison and Ambrose are too high profile for us to manage keeping their deaths a secret. Not that we'd want to. The more coverage there is, the more likely victims will come forward and name names."

"About the coverage…"

"Yes?"

"I want to write the story."

"Will the *Times* allow it?"

I wasn't sure, but tomorrow I'd find out. I'd call my news editor and tell him they would be able to report on the deaths on their own, but to get the full story, they'd need me. I wouldn't accept anything other than my own byline.

"I have to finish what my mother started, Axel, and I can't pass it off to someone else."

"You'll get no argument from me. I don't know what carrot you plan to dangle in front of your bosses, but you can add MI5's cooperation to it."

"Meaning?"

"That exactly, Esland. Full cooperation, but only with you."

"Will MI5 allow it? Or should I be more specific? Will Z allow it?"

"I don't bloody care what Z will or won't allow."

I wondered if Axel knew Z and George had some kind of relationship either presently or in the past. It wasn't something I intended to bring up tonight, but tomorrow I definitely would.

"Do you think he'll offer you the director general position?"

Axel shrugged. "I don't intend to take it if he does."

When I tried to wriggle out of his grasp, he tightened his arms around me.

"I want to run something by you."

"Go ahead."

"I don't know if you're aware, but Wilder and Wren have started their own firm. I may offer my services. What do you think of that idea?"

"Not that it matters what I think, Axel, but I think it's bloody brilliant."

"Good. And it does matter."

He leaned down and kissed me again, this time, deeply. I let my eyes drift closed. With Axel's arms around me, I could sleep.

37

Pinch

When Esland's breathing evened out, I sighed in relief that she'd been able to fall asleep. It was unlikely I'd be able to do the same, but it didn't matter. I had a lot to process, and I could accomplish that with her in my arms.

Fucking Pique. What went down with the man was something I would never forget. I'd made two mistakes. First, I hadn't trusted my instincts until it was almost too late, and that wasn't like me. I'd known as early as that first night when I'd taken Ezzie to Kingham Cross that something was off with Pique.

Next, I'd asked Z to reassign him. I should've known that by then, Pique knew too much. I should've kept the wanker close to monitor him. As it was, I'd given Pique free rein to take what he knew and run with it.

Both of those mistakes could've cost Esland her life, and for that, I'd never forgive myself.

I'd done nearly the same with Westbrook's desk clerk, Hodges. Something had been off with the man, and I'd sicced Pique on his background check. That had been the bloody stupidest thing of them all.

If the stars had aligned perfectly for what went down earlier tonight, I'd played an integral role in seeing to it they did.

None of that could be left out of my report. If Z wasn't already settled on giving the DG job to George, it would clinch it for her. Not that I cared. Like I'd told Esland, if it was offered, I'd decline. I didn't know whether Wilder or Wren would be interested in bringing me on board, but even if they weren't, it wouldn't change my decision about leaving MI5.

I felt Esland's breathing change and her muscles stiffen. I stroked her face and kissed the top of her head. That seemed to be enough to gently coax her out of the nightmare her subconscious was leading her into. For that reason alone, that she might need me to do it again, I wouldn't sleep tonight.

By dawn, I'd not only drafted most of my report in my head, but I also had a plan for how to proceed with the rest of the investigation.

Ezzie had stirred a couple more times, but like the first, I was able to soothe her back into a restful sleep without waking her.

"Good morning," she said in her soft, sweet voice.

I rolled to my side so I could look at her beautiful face. Waking up with her beside me every day for the rest of my life was the only thing I needed to be a very happy man.

I brushed her hair from her face. "How are you feeling?"

"I have a headache, but otherwise, not too bad." She rubbed her wrist where they'd bound her. "A little sore here too."

If they weren't already dead, I would go back and make sure that everyone who had hurt her suffered greatly before knowing they were about to meet their maker.

I hadn't thought much about an afterlife, except with the hope that the evildoers of the world continued to pay the price for their wrongs long after they were dead. In this case, I hoped the men who had kidnapped her spent eternity rotting in hell.

"What are you thinking about?"

I shook my head. "Nothing important."

"You have that look on your face that you used to get when you saw me."

I looked into her eyes. "I'm sorry, Esland, that I ever made you feel as though I didn't like you. I can assure you that my negative feelings weren't as strong as I led you to believe, even if only by my actions. If anything, I was fighting an attraction to you that I didn't understand, or maybe it was more that I didn't allow myself to acknowledge it."

Her gaze continued to stay focused on me.

"It wasn't until the night at the pub when Wilder mentioned your parents—or realized who you were—I can't remember exactly how it went down. I do know this, though. The very moment I realized that we'd known each other years ago, something clicked inside me. I know it sounds beyond ridiculous, but I swear I loved you then, Ezzie."

"I don't think it's so ridiculous."

I smiled. "No? I'm glad to hear it. What I'm trying to tell you though, is there was something about you that unsettled me. I didn't understand it, which made me..."

"An arsehole?"

I laughed out loud. "That is a better word than I would've chosen."

"Not long before the night at the pub, Darrow and I were talking. It was the night when she told me about Wren's true identity. Anyway, she said that if I was ever in trouble, I could trust that you'd help me if I asked you to. It was as though she knew something was on the horizon."

"I must thank her. If she hadn't said that to you, I'm not sure your naked body would be pressed against mine."

Esland wiggled as though she was reinforcing her state of nakedness. Then she grew more serious.

"What do you think of Darrow training here in the States?"

"I think it's a bloody good idea as well as an invaluable opportunity for her."

"Darrow killed Pique," Esland said, barely above a whisper.

"She did. How do you feel about that?"

"I owe her my life. If she hadn't…he wanted them to kill me."

"He was the long-lost other heir. Either that, or he wanted everyone to think he was and somehow believed he could do so."

"That bastard Hodges—he was in on it too."

"Are you ready to talk about what happened?"

"On the record?" she asked.

"It might be best if at least Doc heard your first recounting as well."

"Before we leave this room, there's something else I need to tell you."

"Go ahead." I rested my upper body on my elbow.

"It's about Z and George. I don't know what their relationship is presently, but I saw them. Together."

In the same way Wilder's recognition of who Esland was and that we'd met before had, her words now, sent curious memories flying through my brain. Little things I may never have otherwise remembered, took on an entirely different meaning.

"I'm sorry, Axel."

"What ever are you sorry for?" I asked, jerking my head from where I was looking out the window, to her face.

"You must be disappointed."

"Not in the slightest. In fact, what I'm thinking is maybe I shouldn't consider staying in the spy business. Obvious signs are speeding by me with little or no recognition on my part."

"You're being too hard on yourself."

"Not that it matters, but how do you know about Z and George?"

"I told you, I saw them. I didn't recognize either of them at the time, nor did they recognize me, but when they arrived at Kingham Cross, that night came back to me."

"Did they acknowledge it in any way?"

"I did." She laughed. "I told them I wasn't going to continue to ignore the elephant in the room. George was vexed, but Z found it amusing."

"Sounds like him, although at this point, he has very little to lose. Not so true for George."

"My only concern was—is—for you."

I kissed her. "We should see who else is awake."

"I know." Esland pouted.

"Five more minutes."

"How about fifteen?"

"Let's make it an even thirty," I said, laughing.

38

Esland

I sat next to Axel at the table. Merrigan was on my other side, and Doc sat across from me. Also there, were Edge, Ranger, and Diesel. When I struggled telling them what happened to me, Merrigan reached over and held my hand, squeezing it when I faltered.

Since I'd been unconscious most of the time I was held captive, there wasn't a lot I could add that Axel and the rest didn't already know.

"Where's Darrow?" I asked when I got to the part where my friend had killed Pique.

Merrigan leaned in closer. "She's having a hard time of it this morning. With the job we do, there comes a point when we're forced to take someone's life for the first time. It's hard on everyone."

I nodded in understanding. Darrow had killed a man last night. That it was done to save my life, really had little impact on how hard it must be to realize she'd taken the life of another.

"Quint is with her," Merrigan added.

"What have we learned about the security breach?" Axel asked.

"Damn near flawless takedown of most of our systems. Once again, though, Burns was a step ahead," said Doc.

"Burns?" I asked.

"Kade's father," murmured Merrigan. "Remember, I told you about them."

"Right. Sorry."

Merrigan patted my hand. "With all you've gone through, precious, you're doing remarkably well."

"Burns is a technological savant," Doc said, clearly proud of his father. "While his system wasn't fail-safe, he did work in the necessary components on the back end to allow for this exact scenario."

"Pique would've had access to the system by way of clearances we didn't pull in time. My fault," said Axel.

Everyone at the table either shook their head or murmured their disagreement with Axel's statement.

"There was no reason to suspect the extent of his involvement," said Edge. Something in his voice made me think he felt as guilty about not suspecting the man as Axel did.

"In this case, it was a matter of the fox guarding the hen house," offered Merrigan. "Not the first time, nor the last. As soon as we're better able to recognize them, they come up with new ways to travel in our midst unnoticed."

I wanted to ask if Merrigan spoke from experience, as it sounded, but this wasn't the time. Maybe there would never be a right time for me to ask such a question.

"From what we've learned reading Veronica Cartwright's diaries and by overhearing part of their conversation last night, it is likely Pattison and Ambrose were within the top layer of both the sexual abuse and the doping conspiracies. I believe the crimes are systemic, if not pandemic—as much as I wish it was neither," said Axel.

"There's a good chance the Football Governing Organization is aware of both," added Edge.

Axel checked the time. "MI5 will have done a thorough sweep by now."

All heads turned to Axel.

"I spoke with Z a few minutes before we gathered. He had warrants ready based on the intel he received last night."

I watched as Axel and Kade made eye contact, both nodding in acknowledgment. It was somewhat astounding to me that a privately held, US-owned, covert ops firm worked so closely with SIS. It would be the same if Axel joined on with Wilder and Wren.

It wouldn't be possible for me to write a story about it, as fascinating as it would be for the *Times* readership.

"Z is leaking the deaths of Pattison, Ambrose, and Hodges. The other two men who were involved last night have yet to be identified. Pique's death, on the other hand, will not be addressed presently."

"What about his family?" I asked.

Axel put his hand on mine. "He had none, Ezzie."

I got up from the table and walked toward the back of the house and into the bedroom. Once there, I turned around and walked back to the table where everyone was gathered.

"Where's his body now?"

"At the local morgue," answered Merrigan.

"I want a DNA test."

When Axel said he'd take care of it, all heads turned in his direction a second time, including mine. "You want to know whether you're his family," he murmured.

With tears in my eyes, I nodded. "Thank you," I mouthed.

This time when I got up from the table and walked to the bedroom, I went inside and closed the door behind me. I fell on the bed, clutching the pillow. I heard the door open and close, and then felt the weight of Axel sitting next to me.

"Thank you for understanding."

"Of course."

"To think he may have been the only family I had, and he wanted me dead, all for money." I sobbed harder into the pillow.

"Money can do ugly things to people."

"I don't want it. Not any of it. I'll turn every bit of it over to the government."

"If that's what you want to do, then you should do it."

I sat up and wiped my tears. "You wouldn't try to talk me out of it?"

"Never."

"Even given the sum?"

"I've not seen money deliver happiness, Ezzie. The happiest person I know makes very little, in fact."

"Your father?"

He nodded. "He's never cared a thing about it. I have no idea if he even has savings. The cottage has always been 'his' even though it's part of the Whittaker Estate. He never wants for food or any other necessities. Granted, I would've loved to see him travel, but it wasn't something he wanted."

"You're a good man, Axel Fulton."

"Thank you, sweetness, but it's my father you mean."

"No, I meant you. I wondered, you know, how you felt once you learned that I was Lord Westbrook's great-granddaughter. That, in itself, concerned me. When the solicitor told me the basic details of the trust, I wondered more. I should've known you'd react the way you are."

Axel cocked his head.

"If I denounced it all today, you wouldn't care."

"Why would I, other than you should do what you believe best for you. What you think will make you happy."

"And what if I choose to keep it all? Buy an airplane like the one your friends own?"

"Ezzie, I don't know why you're asking all of these questions. What I do know is, I love you. You. Just you. Not your job or your money. That isn't what defines you. With or without either, you would remain the same person."

"When can we go home?"

He smiled and stroked my cheek with his finger. "Soon. I promise. Z and George"—he wiggled his eyebrows, which made me laugh—"are determining the current threat level. I'll be in constant communication with them, which means as soon as we can return to the UK, we will."

We heard a knock at the door and Darrow's voice from the other side.

"Come in."

"Am I intruding?"

"Yes," Axel said at the same time I said no.

When Darrow took a few more steps into the room, Axel leaned in. "If you'll be all right, I have some phone calls to make."

I smiled. "I'll be fine."

"Don't leave on my account," teased Darrow when he walked out of the room and closed the door behind him.

I patted the bed and Darrow sat down.

"Are you okay?" I asked.

"Me? I wasn't the one kidnapped."

"No, but you were the one who had to kill a man last night. I don't know how to thank you for saving my life."

"I'm okay, True. I promise."

"Merrigan told me you were struggling and that you were with Quint."

"I was with Quint." Darrow winked. "And you know I'm not a morning person. Since he was willing to sleep in, so did I."

"I'm happy for you, Darrow."

"Hold on a minute. Don't forget what I told you the day Axel whisked me away from training to reassure you that I no longer had a claim to stake on him. I told you I was alone because I need to figure out who I am or who I want to be. That hasn't changed."

"Understood," I said, because I did. Completely.

"Plus, I'm leaving with Doc and Merrigan tomorrow."

"You are?"

Darrow nodded. "I'm training with—get this— Leech Hess and Burns Butler."

"I'm guessing those names should mean something to me."

"True, True," said Darrow, shaking her head. "If there was ever a story you should write, and not necessarily for the *Times*. Have you considered writing a book? I'm telling you, look them up."

I laughed at Darrow's enthusiasm. "Wouldn't most of what I might learn about them be classified?"

"Not if you wrote 'fiction.'"

"Maybe I will, then."

"Good. Whenever Axel releases you from protective custody, which may be never, considering he's the one protecting you and I doubt he'll easily relinquish having you by his side twenty-four hours a day. But if he does, you can come visit and interview them."

"I would love that, sincerely."

Darrow stood and so did I.

"I'm happy for you, True. I love that you and Axel are together. It actually gives me hope that one day I'll find true love of my own, and like you just said, I mean that sincerely. Now, this has been fun, but I'm starving. Help me make breakfast?"

39

Pinch

I was ending my call with Z when I saw Ezzie come out of the bedroom following Darrow. When she smiled, my heart skipped a beat. How could I have been so daft to not realize straightaway that she owned my heart?

Z's report was that while they hadn't yet found evidence of a cover-up of either the sex abuse or doping, as soon as Pattison's and Ambrose's deaths were announced, "whistleblowers" started coming from every direction.

"You're safe to return to England," were Z's last words before I heard the familiar chimes indicating the call was over.

"Great news," I whispered in Ezzie's ear when she wrapped her arms around my waist. "We can leave for London tomorrow."

She pulled back. "We can?"

"Z assures me the coast is clear."

"He's probably just saying that because I know his secret and if a footballer offs me, he won't have to worry about me exposing George and him."

"Actually, he asked if we'd like to have dinner with them sometime next week."

"You're joking."

I laughed and shook my head. "I'm not. I promise he issued the invitation."

"What about the DG job?"

"I told him earlier I was withdrawing my name from consideration." Z had feigned disappointment, but the truth was, he was the one who'd initially assumed I was leaving.

"How did he take it?"

"He expected it. He's also expecting my resignation once this case wraps up. We're negotiating that aspect of it right now."

"No longer at Her Majesty's service, then?"

"On the contrary, I always will be. For the rest of my life, honestly. The roles may change, but I chose to serve the Crown, Ezzie. I'll not go back on the promise I made."

She put her arms around my neck. "I'd never ask that of you."

"I love you." I rested my forehead against hers, wishing we were already back in the UK so I could say the words I really longed to.

40

Pinch

"They're falling like flies," Z said as we drove from Heathrow to Whittaker Abbey. "So far the majority of the Football Governing Organization's body has resigned. Many of whom are also under investigation."

"You have my report," I said.

"I do. If we need to question Miss Cartwright, I'll let you know."

"If you decide it's necessary, I'll be the one conducting the interrogation."

"Bloody hell, Pinch. It wouldn't be an interrogation."

"If it involves Ezzie, I'm in charge."

Z's laughter rang through the mobile's speaker. "Good luck with that."

"Wilder and Wren will be back by this time next week," he said after ending the call.

"Already? That was quick, wasn't it?"

"It almost seems a lifetime ago that they left."

I pulled through the gates of the estate where I grew up, and a sense of peace washed over me. This was home to me, and if everything went as planned, it would also be where Ezzie and I began our life together.

"There's a beautiful woman," my father said, coming out to greet us when we stopped in front of his cottage.

"Hi, Pops," I said, hugging him. "It's so good to see you."

"You too, son," my father said, looking into my eyes and slipping something into my pocket.

"Hello, Wellie," Esland said.

I watched as she and my father embraced.

"Come in out of the cold." He led us inside.

"Actually, I have one quick thing I need to do. Ezzie, will you be okay on your own for a bit?"

"I'll hardly be on my own, Axel. Your father and I will visit."

"Of course." I kissed her cheek first and then squeezed my father's shoulder before walking out.

"Welcome back, Pinch," said Shiver when we met in the abbey's entryway and embraced.

"Thanks. Can you spare a minute?"

"Always." Shiver motioned to the drawing room. Once inside, he closed the door. "Fancy a brandy?"

"Always," I repeated with a wink.

"Tell me what's on your mind, Axel," Shiver said as we both took a seat.

"You once made me an offer regarding Bristol House."

Shiver nodded. "An open offer."

"I'd like to take you up on it."

Shiver jumped up and shook my hand. "I'm so pleased, truly. This is wonderful news." He poured each of us another round and sat back down. "You know the state it's in."

I nodded. "I'm well aware, and I want you to know how much I appreciate your generosity."

"You are and always have been my second brother. I don't think any of us have kept our affection for you and Wellie a secret." Shiver brushed his finger over his lower lip. "Will the fair Ms. Cartwright be moving in as well?"

"I'd rather say Mrs. Fulton."

"Well done, mate. Well done." Shiver was standing again, and this time I did too.

"I may be optimistic in my confidence that she'll agree." I pulled out the box my father had slipped into my pocket and showed its contents to Shiv.

"It was your mother's, no?" he asked.

"Do you think she'll like it? It's rather modest."

"Modest? No, Axel, it's the opposite. There are few symbols, if any, richer with love than that ring."

"Thank you." I'd been worried that maybe Ezzie would want something more lavish, but Shiver's words rang true. "I'm off."

"Celebration dinner tomorrow night, then?"

"I'll let you know," I answered sheepishly.

"And I'll let Mrs. Mollybock know to prepare a feast." Shiver shook his head. "Perhaps I should have Losha ask. Although, if it's a dinner in your and Esland's honor, she'll likely agree even if the request is delivered by me."

I laughed. I'd never understood Mrs. Mollybock's evident dislike of the current Duke of Bedfordshire. Perhaps later, I'd ask my father. Now, though, I had a far more important question to ask.

41

Esland

I was laughing when I heard the door open and Axel come in.

"Are you telling stories, Pops?" he asked.

"I understand you once thought it a good idea to bring a beehive into your sleeping quarters." I could barely get the words out without laughing.

"Thanks, Pops," I heard him say, and looked over to see the love mirrored in the eyes of father and son. Axel turned to me. "Fancy a drive?"

I was about to point out that we'd just arrived, but decided that no matter where or when Axel asked me to go with him, I'd do so gladly. "Of course."

"We'll be back," Axel said to his father, who smiled and nodded.

"There's something I'd like to show you," he said once we were in the 4x4.

"I can't wait."

"You really can't, can you?"

"I know if there's something you want me to see, it'll be special."

We'd only made two turns when I knew where we were headed. Moments later, we pulled up in front of Bristol House. It had always been my favorite of the three manor houses on the estate.

Axel came around and opened my door, taking my hand and leading me through the gate. He stopped before we reached the front door and cupped my cheek. "Do you have any idea how much I love you?"

"Not more than I love you."

Axel dropped to one knee and took my left hand in his right. "Esland Cartwright, would you please make me the happiest man alive by agreeing to be my wife?"

"Oh, Axel," I gasped, my eyes filling with tears. "Yes, yes, yes. I would love to be your wife. It would make me the happiest woman on earth."

"This belonged to my mother," he said as he slipped a ring on my finger. "It fits perfectly," he whispered in awe. "But if you'd like to pick out something else—"

I silenced him with a kiss. "There's no better ring to be found, Axel. I love it so much." Set in the gold of the ring was the most beautiful ruby I'd ever seen. "I'm humbled to wear it."

He turned toward the house and waved his hand. "What would you think—"

"*Yes!*" I exclaimed, throwing my arms around his neck.

Axel laughed. "You don't know what I was going to say."

"You're asking if I'd like to live in Bristol House, and my answer is yes. A thousand times yes."

"It's a bit neglected."

"A good cleaning is all it needs."

"When's the last time you were in it?"

"The same year you last slayed a dragon on my behalf."

I pulled him toward the front door, but he stopped me before I could go inside. He scooped me in his arms before putting the skeleton key in the keyhole.

As he carried me over the threshold, I kissed him— my future husband, the man I'd loved most of my life, the man who would become my family, and with whom I'd have a flock of children, if he was willing.

"What are you thinking at this moment, my sweet Ezzie?" He set me on my feet once we were inside.

"There are five bedrooms."

"If I remember right, there are six."

"I was thinking we should fill them all with little Ezzies and Axels."

"I would love nothing more, and I can't wait to get started."

I realized I'd been holding my breath waiting for his response. "I can't wait either," I said, pulling him over to the staircase.

As we surveyed both of the main floors, Axel's dismay at the house's state was equal to my enthusiasm and excitement. I'd often wondered why neither Sutton nor Darrow chose this house over Dorchester and Covington. This was far and away the largest and, in my opinion, had the best location.

There was something about it that spoke to me, even as a little girl. I couldn't explain it, but it was as though I knew I'd live in it one day.

We were walking out of the kitchen and into a bedroom just off it when Axel stopped.

"If it comes to it, given my father's age and precarious health, I may ask you to allow him to live with us."

"Allow him? Oh, Axel, do you not know I'd do anything for you and for Wellie? You're my family."

Axel turned his head, but not before I saw tears fill his eyes. I put my hand on his chin and reached up to kiss him.

He smiled. "You are a welcome addition, my sweet Ezzie. It's just been Wellie and me for most of my life."

"What would you think of marrying here?" I laughed at the look on his face. "I promise you, it isn't as bad as it looks. We'll make it a home, Axel."

"I would do anything for you, Esland. Even marry in this dilapidated, old house that we once believed was haunted."

I laughed again and kissed him. "It's where I fell in love with you and knew you'd forever be my protector, slaying all my dragons."

Epilogue

Esland

Six months later

"You are gorgeous, True," said Darrow when she walked into the bedroom where Merrigan and I were finishing dressing.

"Isn't she, though?" Merrigan brushed a lock of hair from my forehead. "The perfect bride."

"I can't believe what you've done with this place, either. The gardens are spectacular."

I laughed. "That's all due to Wellie, and you know it. I did almost nothing."

"And the house itself looks so beautiful."

I did have to admit, Darrow was right. It had come together exactly as I'd imagined it would when Axel and I first walked its floors the day he proposed.

"It's time," Merrigan announced, ushering us from the bedroom.

"Thank you both for being here today."

"Wouldn't have missed it for anything," said Darrow, wiping away a tear.

"Me either," added Merrigan.

Axel and I had agreed to wed in the front garden, where he stood waiting by its gate, along with Sutton, the duke, and the vicar.

A violinist began to play as Merrigan walked down the path, followed by Darrow. When Wellie held his arm out to me, I wrapped mine in it.

"Thank you for walking with me," I whispered.

"I've had no greater honor in my life."

I smiled and turned to where Axel waited. My eyes never left his as I walked toward him.

"I love you," he whispered when I stood beside him.

"And I love you."

The vicar cleared his throat. "Today we are gathered to join together in marriage Axel Andrew Fulton and Esland Victoria Cartwright…"

Keep reading for a preview
of the next book in the
the Royal Agents of MI6 Series—
the The Rancher and the Lady!

Prologue

Quint

January

I stretched my arms above my head and looked out at the sunrise. Typically, I'd be out, riding the ranch by now, but today, my crew was handling the morning chores on their own.

Before coming in last night, I'd asked my men to cover for me. I hadn't needed to explain why; they all knew the mahogany-haired beauty asleep next to me was on the ranch and had been for the last three days.

They spared me the jabs they would've shared with one another under the same circumstances, perhaps sensing the woman was more than a warm body to keep me company on a cold night.

In her sleep, she'd kicked off the blankets and sheet, so her luscious body was on full display, illuminated by the bronze, orange, and yellow hues of the sun's rays streaming in through the window.

The last time she came to visit, she stayed three months but only spent half of that time in my bed.

Later this morning, she'd be leaving, and I wasn't sure she'd ever be back.

Deep inside, part of me wanted to ask her to stay, but we both knew I never would. If Darrow Whittaker ever decided she wanted more than a few laughs coupled with the best sex I'd ever had in my life, she knew where to find me. I couldn't promise I'd be sitting around, waiting on her, though.

"I thought we were sleeping in," she groaned in her sexier-than-shit English accent. When she covered her eyes with her forearm, I couldn't help but lean over and lave the nipple that was now pointed directly at me.

"God, Quint." Darrow's groan turned into a moan as she held my head to her breast.

"Are you sore, baby?" I asked, moving one hand lower.

She shook her head.

"Not good enough. Let me hear the words."

This time, instead of a groan or moan, Darrow growled. When I laughed, she smacked my arm, which only made me laugh harder.

She pushed me until I was on my back and nipped at my neck before trailing her lips down my body.

"Shadow," I said in my most menacing tone.

"I'm leaving today, Quint. If I'm sore, I'll recover."

I pulled her up the front of my body so her chin rested on my sternum. "Let's shower."

"Showering means getting out of bed."

I rolled so she was under me, and then stood. "My understanding was that you had an early flight."

She stuck out her lower lip in a pout. "I do, which is why I don't want to waste time now."

"I like the idea of leaving you wanting more," I said, walking from the bed into the en suite bathroom.

About the Author

USA Today and Amazon Top 15 Bestselling Author Heather Slade writes shamelessly sexy, edge-of-your seat romantic suspense.

She gave herself the gift of writing a book for her own birthday one year. Forty-plus books later (and counting), she's having the time of her life.

The women Slade writes are self-confident, strong, with wills of their own, and hearts as big as the Colorado sky. The men are sublimely sexy, seductive alphas who rise to the challenge of capturing the sweet soul of a woman whose heart they'll hold in the palm of their hand forever. Add in a couple of neck-snapping twists and turns, a page-turning mystery, and a swoon-worthy HEA, and you'll be holding one of her books in your hands.

She loves to hear from my readers. You can contact her at heather@heatherslade.com

To keep up with her latest news and releases, please visit her website at www.heatherslade.com to sign up for her newsletter.

MORE FROM AUTHOR HEATHER SLADE